All The Fixin'

Published by Phaze Books
Also by Marie Rochelle

My Deepest Love: Zack

Caught

PHAZE
Cincinnati, Ohio

www.Phaze.com

All The Fixin'

a novel of erotic romance by

MARIE ROCHELLE

A Phaze Production

Cincinnati, Ohio

Phaze Books
6470A Glenway Avenue, #109
Cincinnati, OH 45211-5222
Phaze is an imprint of Mundania Press, LLC.

To order additional copies of this book, contact:
books@phaze.com
www.Phaze.com

Cover art © 2007 Debi Lewis
Edited by Kathryn Lively

Trade Paperback ISBN-13: 978-1-59426-688-1

First Print Edition – June, 2008
Printed in the United States of America

10 9 8 7 6 5 4 3 2 1

Chapter One

"I can't believe this shit!" Craig growled, jumping up from his seat and slapping his hand on the polished table. "I know she did something to trick my aunt into signing those papers."

"Please take your seat, Mr. Evans. I won't have that kind of outburst again in my office," Mr. Terry threatened, pushing his glasses back up his nose. "This will contains your aunt's final wishes, unless you can prove she wasn't of sound mind when she wrote it."

Craig Evans fell back into his seat and glared across the table at the woman he had grown to hate over the last two years of his aunt's life.

"Fine, don't worry, Mr. Terry. I'll find a way to prove that Miss Anderson isn't the nice, sweet woman she's pretending to be. She used my dying aunt's kindness to get her money."

"Mr. Evans, once again I ask that you please refrain from saying nasty comments about Miss Anderson," Mr. Terry said. "She has been sitting here without saying a word for the past hour. Maybe you could learn something from her."

Craig narrowed his eyes at his nemesis sitting across from him at the table. Sure, she would be quiet and not stir up any trouble. Why would she after his aunt left her in charge of an estate worth over six million dollars? She would never have to work again.

Today she was playing the role of grieving friend, wearing a slim black dress that molded her curves. Subconsciously his gaze was drawn to the small silt in the front, just revealing a hint of rich, Hershey chocolate skin. She even had pulled her shoulder length bob haircut back into a tight bun, displaying her jawbone. He had to give her credit, Shea Anderson looked devastated about the passing of his Aunt Rebecca, but he didn't trust her as far as he could throw her.

How did she not know his aunt was the founder of the firming and plumping lipstick chain? *Luscious Lips* had been in his family for years, and he was the only living relative. How in the hell didn't he get the company? He was close to his aunt, so there was no way she wouldn't have left it to him. No, Shea did something to trick his aunt, and he would find out what it was.

"Mr. Evans, are you listening?" his aunt's lawyer interrupted, making him push thoughts of Shea to the back of his mind, but only for the moment.

"Sorry, Mr. Terry, my mind was somewhere else for a few moments. I apologize," he answered, "Can you repeat what you just said?"

Mr. Terry pushed his glasses up for the fourth time today, then shifted his gaze from him back over to Shea before he continued. "Your aunt left a clause in the will."

"Thank God!" he burst out, happy his Aunt Rebecca hadn't been completely fooled by the sexy siren in front of him.

"Craig, I'm not going to warn you again about speaking your mind. One more comment and I'm done reading this will," Mr. Terry threatened.

"I apologize. I swear that was my last outburst."

"It better be," Mr. Terry said. "The clause in your aunt's will stipulates that Ms. Anderson has until Thanksgiving to turn down the estate. If Shea doesn't claim it, the estate automatically goes to you with no questions asked."

Craig knew there was no way in hell Shea was going to turn down that kind of money. Someone like her had finally found the pot of gold at the end of the rainbow, and giving it back certainly wouldn't enter her mind.

"Mr. Terry, I don't want Rebecca's money. I didn't become her friend for that," Shea's raspy voice interrupted, making him looking back at the woman who had tormented him for months. "I'll sign them over to Craig right now."

"I'm sorry, Miss. Anderson, but you can't sign the papers until then."

"Okay...then I'll be back in touch with you in a couple of weeks," she said, surprising Craig. What was she up to now?

Craig watched as Shea grabbed her jacket off the back of the chair and made her way toward the door. He hated how he noticed everything was perfect on her five-feet, five-inch frame. She didn't even glance in his direction as she went past his chair, out the door.

"Craig, don't you bully her into not taking the estate," his aunt's lawyer warned him as he gathered up the will and other papers off the desk. "Rebecca had her mind up until the day she died. If she left Shea all that money it was for a reason. Now it's up to you to find out why."

"The only thing I have to do is be here on the day Shea signs over what's belongs to me," Craig stated, getting up from his seat. He left with room without a backward glance in his aunt's lawyer's direction.

* * * *

Shea Anderson shoved her arms into the sleeves of her jacket and buttoned it, wishing the elevator would hurry up. She didn't have any more energy to go another round with Craig. It took all her willpower not to stare at him during the will reading.

Craig Evans wouldn't want her drooling all over him. He'd made it clear when he visited his aunt that she wasn't his type of woman. No, Craig always brought the leggy strawberry blondes with him— model types who would always be a size zero no matter how much they ate or didn't eat, who had men like Craig dying to be with them.

Why did she have to be attracted to a man who thought she befriended his aunt for her money? God, he wouldn't believe she didn't know who Rebecca Anderson was until his aunt had told her two weeks ago. Rebecca said that she was leaving her something in her will, but her six-million dollar estate never crossed her mind. Hell, she thought it was going to be the silver Jaguar she loved driving so much.

Leaning her shoulder against the wall by the slow moving elevator, she massaged her temples with the tips of her fingers. This day couldn't get any worse for her.

"Don't stand there and act all innocent when we both know you're counting the days until you have all of that money," a deep timber voice accused.

Pivoting, she threw Craig a hateful look and prayed he wouldn't notice the crush she had on him. Today his dark brown hair was styled back off his forehead and the ends were touched the collar of his white suit. The dark blue suit molded the perfect body she knew he worked out five days a week to keep.

She dropped her gaze down to his full, firm lips, dreaming what it would be like if he ever pushed down the hate he harbored for her and kissed her. Shea quickly shook the thought from her mind. Craig detested her and didn't mince his words about it.

"Mr. Evans, aren't you late for a corporate meeting or something?" Shea sighed and faced the elevator door.

"Shea, don't you ignore me." Craig said behind her.

Craig wrapped his fingers around her arm and made her face him. He pulled her so close to him that her breasts brushed the hardness of his chest. She bit the inside of her lip to keep from moaning as the unexpected electricity charged through her body. Her eyes darted up to Craig's face to see if he felt the same thing, but she only saw his same hard look.

"I won't let you steal my aunt's money. You aren't part of the family and never will be. That money should have gone to me to pass on to my future wife and kids."

Shaking off Craig's touch, she folded her arms under her breasts. "You'll get your wish on

Thanksgiving, but until then stay out of my way, Mr. Anderson," she shot back as the elevator's door slid open behind her. "I want your aunt's money as about as much as I want to be in a relationship with your arrogant ass." With that finally comment hanging in the air between them, Shea got on the elevator. It closed before Craig had a chance to retort.

Chapter Two

"How did the will reading go?" Josh leaned against the door frame of Craig's office. "Was Shea there? Did you get into another fight with her? Was she wearing something sexy and hot?"

Craig set down the graphic design report he was reading and looked up at his business partner for the past ten years. Josh didn't hide the fact that he thought Shea was gorgeous, and Craig hated how that bothered him. Shea didn't need to get hooked up with his friend. Josh would date a woman for a few months then toss her to the side when a better one came along.

"I didn't pay attention to what Shea was wearing," he lied, remembering how the black dress fit Shea like a glove. He wondered if she even wore underwear today because he didn't notice a panty line when she got on the elevator.

"Sure you didn't. Haven't you been lusting after her ever since you saw her swimming in the pool at your aunt's house?" Josh laughed. "You get a hard on when she gets within twenty feet of you."

"You don't know what you're talking about. I'm not attracted to Shea Anderson in any way, shape, or form. She can rot in hell for all I care. All I want her to do is sign over my aunt's estate to me. If I don't see her after that, I'll die a happy man."

"You are in such denial about Shea. Don't you realize that you haven't been out on a real date in months? All those girls you dragged to your aunt's house were only arm pieces to get a reaction out of Shea. But she never once fell for your trap."

"Josh, don't you have a program to design or something? For the last time, I don't have any feelings for Shea Anderson and I never will," Craig denied.

"Great," Josh grinned, moving away from the door, "now I don't have any guilt about asking her out on a date."

"Don't you dare ask Shea out," he yelled, but his friend had already left. "Shit, I can't let Shea accept Josh's date." He didn't have time to think about why it bothered him so much. Craig reached for the phone at the same time it rung, and he cursed at whoever was on the other end.

"Hello," he snapped.

* * * *

Shea wandered along the walking trail until she came upon her special spot. Kicking off her shoes, she folded her legs underneath her, then, pulled a bag of bread crumbs from her purse to feed the ducks. Tossing a handful to the animals, she mulled over the huge mess that had been dropped into her lap.

Why did Rebecca do this to her? She was fine working as a data entry clerk for the local insurance agency. The weekly pay was good and she didn't need Craig breathing down her neck every minute until Thanksgiving rolled around. She wouldn't be in this situation if she hadn't felt a connection with Rebecca the first day she walked into her job.

She had met Rebecca about three years ago when she came into Shea's office to get more life insurance. For some odd reason they started talking about Shea's plants and struck up an instant friendship. Rebecca was outspoken, a quality Shea didn't have but hoped to achieve after spending time with her newfound friend.

Rebecca had a zest for life that she never had found in her twenty-nine years. Shea seriously doubted she would have crossed paths with Rebecca if it hadn't been for her job. One of her friends from college recommended her for the agency because her boyfriend's brother was looking for someone. After two interviews with the Mr. Clean look-a-like, she finally landed the position and the rest was history.

Anytime she ran into a problem or situation that she couldn't handle, Rebecca was only a phone call away. After talking with her for an hour or however long it took, things became better for her. Rebecca was the grandmother she had always wanted as a child, since both her grandmothers died before she was born.

Craig Evans never wanted to understand the special bond she had shared with his wonderful aunt. From the first day when Craig saw her outside by the pool, he acted like she wasn't worthy of even breathing the same air as him.

Shea lost count of how many times Rebecca tried to throw her and Craig together, from running errands for her or spending time in the kitchen cooking meals for her. Rebecca hinted how she wanted her nephew to settle down with a good woman, and Rebecca must have thought she was that woman. A week before she died, Rebecca hinted she would end up a part of the family no matter how long it took.

She knew the only way that would happen was for Craig to fall in love with her and propose. Since she knew that Craig wasn't mentally ill or on drugs, Rebecca's wish would never come true.

Her friend Rebecca had been such a romantic, always watching the old black and white movies, but Shea couldn't hold onto the illusion Craig that would ever look at her like that. They weren't compatible no matter how much Shea longed for them to be.

"Rebecca, why did you do this to me," she asked aloud. "You had to have known I wouldn't take a cent of your money." Shea sighed and gave the ducks the last of the bread crumbs. Brushing her hands off, Shea slipped her shoes back on then got up from the bench.

Chapter Three

Two days later Shea sat at her desk and stared at the man seated across from her. She was confused and a little stunned by the fact that he was even there. "Why do you think you can you tell me whom I can and can't go out on a date with, Mr. Evans?" she asked, twirling the pencil around on her desk. She had been flabbergasted to find her nemesis waiting for her outside her job this morning.

What was he up to now? She wasn't going to change her mind about the money, so why was he acting all concerned about her well-being? If Josh ever called and asked her out on a date, it wasn't any of Craig's business what her answer would be.

"I just think with everything you have in your life right now, Accepting on a date with Josh wouldn't be in your best interest," Craig responded.

"Don't lie to me. You're only here to hint around to see if I've changed my mind about not taking your aunt's estate." She denied hating how Craig seemed more masculine in the small confines of her office.

"Shea, you think you know me so well, don't you? I might actually be concerned that Josh only wants to use you for another purpose."

She stopped twirling the pencil and folded her hands on the desk, ignoring the ringing of the phone by her elbow. "Why in the world would Josh want to use me? We have only spoken to each other the few times he came to your aunt's house with you. Is it so hard to believe that he might find me attractive and want to ask me out?"

"Yes, I find that hard to believe," Craig said. "Josh would never ask you out on a date."

Once, a comment like that from Craig would have hurt, but she was used to his parting shots by now. "Don't worry about me, Craig. We only have to deal with each other for a little while longer and then I'll never darken your doorstep again."

"Who in the world is calling me?" Shea said, picking up the phone. "Lester Insurance, Shea speaking. How may I help you?" She took a quick glance at Craig, then spun her chair around away from him.

"Hello, Josh. Yes, I do remember who you are. You want to know if I'm free tonight for dinner and a movie? I'm surprised that you called me. I didn't think I was your type," Shea answered, watching Craig's face in the mirror behind her desk. "Oh, someone just mentioned you don't go out with women like me."

She laughed as Josh flirted with her over the phone. "Thanks for the compliment. I think I'm pretty hot myself." Shea waited and gave Josh's dinner invitation some thought. Something was going on between Craig and Josh, and she wanted to get to the bottom of it. "Sure, I'd love to have dinner with you. I'm with someone right now, so can you call me back later and I'll give you directions to my house. Bye."

Shea disconnected the call and took another peek at the mirror. The hurt look in Craig's eyes made her hesitate, but she quickly shook it as a trick of the eye. Craig wouldn't care if she went out with his business partner.

Spinning back around in the chair, she hung up the phone. "Is there anything else I can do for you, Craig?"

"I can't believe you're actually going out on a date with Josh. You know nothing about him."

"That's why people go out on dates, to learn about the other person," Shea replied.

"You wouldn't have gone out on a date with me if I had asked you," Craig pointed out. He leaned toward her desk, showing off tanned skin exposed by opened collar of his button-down shirt..

Don't drool and keep your composure. This is a trick, don't fall for it.

"Craig, what kind of game are you playing with me?" She got up from her desk and went around it, stopping by the edge. She stared down at Craig, trying to figure out what was going on in his mind. "We aren't friends. To be honest, we aren't even acquaintances, so why the fake interest in my love life?"

"I've seen Josh in action over the years. I may not be your biggest fan, but I don't want Josh using you. My aunt was fond of you and she would be upset if I didn't try to warn you away from my partner." Craig watched her, like he could see right inside her soul.

Shea ran Craig's answer in her head until she finally realized what he was trying to say. "You don't want me to go out with Josh because you're afraid."

Bedroom eyes blinked a couple of times before they stared at her point blank. "What am I afraid of, Miss Anderson?" Craig demanded, standing up.

Squaring her shoulders, she gave Craig a long stare to top his bullying one. She was tired of having a crush on a man who hated her one second and tried to run her life the next. "You're worried that Josh and I will hit it off, and if we do I'll still be a part of your life."

"You can't be seriously thinking about looking at Josh as a possible boyfriend?" Craig laughed. "He can't even commit to a brand of toothpaste for longer than two weeks."

"Why shouldn't I?" she taunted. "Josh is a handsome and successful man. Maybe I'll find out what else lies beneath the surface."

"With Josh what you see if what you get. He doesn't have any deeper layers to him." Craig moved closer to her. "He dates women for sport, not to form a meaningful connection."

Craig was about to invade her personal space, so she stuck out her hands and tried to stop him, but her hand ended up pressed against his starched shirt right above his heart. She was too shocked to move. Craig's heart was beating a mile a minute. Was she the cause of it? Could Craig be jealous at the thought of her going out with another man?

"You're jealous," she blurted.

"Shea, the only thing I'm jealous of is you having control of my aunt's estate, and after you sign it over to me I won't have any feelings for you whatsoever." Craig brushed her hands off his chest and left her office without a backwards glance in her direction.

* * * *

In the parking lot, Craig fumbled with his key four times before finally getting it into the lock. Sliding into the car, he turned on the air conditioner to full blast and prayed it would cool down the heat in his body. He was thankful he didn't lose it back in Shea's office. How did she not know how much he wanted her? That was the only reason Josh called to ask her out.

Josh could push all he wanted, but he wasn't about to admit he had unrequited love for Shea since the moment he laid eyes on her. Some of his married friends, whom he didn't talk to anymore, would laugh their heads off if they could see him now. He had constantly teased them about how their women had them wrapped around their fingers and vowed it would never happen to him.

Now the woman he might be ready to settle down with was about to go out on a date with his business partner.

"I can't let this happen," Craig screamed, banging his hand on the dashboard. "Shea won't fall for Josh. I'll make sure of that."

Craig took some time to get his anger under control before he drove out of the parking lot. He had a lot of things to get done. He was still in the dark about when the date was actually going to take place.

Chapter Four

"Josh, are you sure you want to go out with me for the right reasons?" Shea asked over the phone, adding a pinch of seasoning to the sauce boiling on top of the stove. "I'm beginning to have second thoughts about this. Craig hates me, and I don't think he's going to like the thought of me going out on a date with his best friend."

"Craig doesn't have a say in what we do." Josh pointed out. "How can we get to know each other better if we don't have a nice dinner?"

"You never seemed interested in me until Craig's aunt left me all that money. I'm not going to keep it. So, if you're looking for an easy life you won't find it with me."

"Who told you I wanted to be a kept man?" Josh said, insulted. "I love working, and the thought of a woman supporting me never crossed my mind. Who told you that lie?"

Shea felt like a world class idiot for even opening her mouth about what Craig hinted to in her office early today. Why was she allowing him to run her life? "Umm...I can't tell you."

"Don't worry, I can guess. It was C.C. wasn't it?"

She laughed at Josh calling Craig by his nickname. "Craig would never let me call him that."

"Why not? Aren't the two of you sorta friends because of his Aunt Rebecca?"

She stirred the sauce two more times before she turned it off and placed it on the other side of the stove, off the heat. "Where did you get that idea? Craig can't stand me, and is counting the days until I'm out of his life for good," Shea admonished. "The only reason he's talking to me now is to make sure I sign those papers on Thanksgiving Day."

"You don't understand how Craig's mind works."

"What makes you think I want to understand how Craig Clark Evans' mind works for in the first place?" She grabbed a plate for the chicken pesto she was having tonight for dinner.

"Because you're in love with him, and I believe C.C. feels the same way about you."

Shea narrowly missed dropping the plate on the floor as Josh's words rung in her ears. She laid the plate back down on the counter, then went across the room and took a seat in front of her bay window. "Have you lost your mind? Craig isn't in love with me. I'm sure the word *love* and my name have never crossed his mind."

"All right, if Craig isn't in love with you, then why did he warn you not to go out on a date with me?"

Giggling, Shea folded her legs yoga style and rested her back against the window. "Craig didn't want me around him after the thing with his aunt's will is over. It was more for his benefit then either of ours."

"No, I don't believe that. I've known C.C. for years, and the second I mentioned how hot I thought you were he almost took my head off."

Josh wasn't thinking straight. Craig wasn't in love with her. Hell, the only person Craig probably loved was himself. There was just something about the way Craig acted that didn't scream marriage to her if he decided to walk down the aisle it wouldn't be with her.

"Josh, can we stop talking about Craig?" She sighed. "I thought you called about our date next week."

"Shea, if things work out the way I plan, I won't be the one going out on that date with you in seven days," Josh hinted, then hung up on her.

"Don't you dare do anything," she yelled into her end of the phone. "Do you hear me?"

* * * *

Craig paced back and forth inside the office while he dialed the cell phone number for the fourth time in less than twenty minutes. He hated to be kept waiting, and Josh knew that. Where the hell was he?

He stopped dead in his tracks as a thought popped into his head. No, he wasn't going to let his mind travel down that road. Pushing the unwanted idea away he pressed the speed dial on his phone again. The phone rang another six times with no answer.

Snapping the phone shut, he shoved it into his front slacks pocket. "They aren't out a date together." Josh was only joking around when he said he would like to date Shea. His best friend was as bad as his Aunt Rebecca when it came to Shea and him.

What had his aunt been thinking about bring someone like Shea into his life? She reminded him so much of Olivia and how he ruined things with the girl that loved him all those years ago in college.

Olivia had the same beautiful skin tone and huge brown eyes that he had got lost in every chance he got. She had believed in him even when he hadn't. She stayed up late with him, drinking coffee and studying for classes that weren't even hers, just to help him get a passing grade.

Back then he had the best woman a man could ask for, until she caught him kissing his lab partner in his dorm room. No matter how many times he had tried to apologize with gifts, flowers, or cards for his stupidity, Olivia wouldn't listen to him. She even missed her college graduation to avoid having contact with him.

He thought he wouldn't meet another woman like Olivia until Shea stole his breath at his aunt's house. She possessed everything he loved in a woman. She had a quiet strength that only showed itself when it was needed, honesty, and a depth most of the woman he had run-ins with lacked.

Shea didn't know the reasons he was always picking on her but, God rest her soul, Aunt Rebecca called him on it numerous times. She was the only person in his family that he confided in about his past with Olivia. His aunt was a second mother to him after his parents died, after he graduated from college. He still missed the hell out of both of them, and he knew if he had told them about Olivia they wouldn't have cared. They always wanted the best for him, and for a second time in his life he was about to lose that.

"I won't let Josh have her," Craig promised himself.

"Won't let me have who?" Josh asked, sneaking up behind him.

Spinning around, Craig leveled his soon-to-be best friend with an unblinking stare. "Where have you been for the past two hours, and the name Shea better not leave your mouth."

Chapter Five

Dear Journal,

Today turned out a lot differently than I thought it would. Craig came to see me at work, looking as handsome as ever. I had my hand clenched in my lap to keep from brushing back that lock of hair resting above his left eyebrow.

I have it so bad for this man that I almost make myself sick. All he has to do is walk into a room and I don't see anyone else.

Shea drummed her purple pen against the sheets in her journal as she thought back to everything that happened with Craig today. A part of her thought it was juvenile to keep a journal at twenty-nine, but the creative side of her loved ending her nights like this. She had started writing two nights after Rebecca introduced her to Craig. She could never let Rebecca know she had crush on her nephew, so putting pen to paper became the next best thing.

Slipping a Hershey's Kiss into her mouth, she stretched out on the bed and finished writing down her thoughts:

I couldn't believe that he actually came to my job to warn me against Josh. Why does he care who I go out on a date with? For a fast second I thought he might be jealous, but the idea left the second I spoke it out loud. Like usual, Craig laughed and made it out to be something different.

He's only interested in his aunt's estate and nothing else. Once he has that paper in his hand, Craig "C.C." Clark Evans will forget my name. So why does the thought of that put a deep pain in my heart?

Closing the book, Shea opened the drawer by her bed and laid it inside, then closed the door. Sitting up on the bed, she quickly braided her hair, then slid between the covers. She couldn't keep thinking about Craig and the lack of love he had for her. Tomorrow she had to go in early because her boss was out of town and it was Friday. She sent up a silent prayer she didn't lose her mind with any of the crazy clients she might have to deal with.

Chapter Six

"You haven't said a word to me all day. Does that mean you're still pissed at me?" Craig saved the cover art he was working on and glanced at Josh, positioned in front of his desk. Josh never gave him a straight answer about where he had been the other day. He couldn't ask Shea if he was with her because that would send up a red flag.

He had tried two or three ways to get a direct answer out of Josh, but it wasn't working. His friend was more secretive, and nothing he said or did was going to change it.

"What do you think?" he replied. "You're pursuing a woman that I told you not to."

"Is it because you want Shea for yourself?" Josh hinted.

"We have gone over that and you already have the answer to that question." Craig didn't want Josh in a relationship with Shea for a lot of reasons, his being in love with her was the biggest one. "You know how I feel about her. Why do you keep asking me?"

"I'm going to keep asking until you admit the words. Do you want to lose her like you did Olivia all those years ago?"

Craig rose from his seat and came around the desk. "Olivia is part of my past and I regret what I did to her. But I won't make the same mistake with Shea. I'm not cheating on her with another woman."

"You can't cheat on someone you aren't in a relationship with. Shit, man, you can't even admit that you're in love with her aloud," Josh complained, moving away from him.

"I'm working up to the relationship part. Why don't you butt out and give me some time to think about this?" He sighed, running his fingers through his hair. "I need time to do this the right way or Shea won't believe my feelings are real."

"The right way," Josh scoffed, making him fight down the urge to punch in friend in the face. "Man, if you wait any longer Shea will be married to someone else."

"Josh, I'm not playing with you. Leave her alone," Craig threatened. "She's meant to be with me and it's going to happen."

Josh lifted his hand between them, brushing off his comment. "Yeah, I'll believe that when I see it. Because at this moment Shea doesn't know how she feels about you."

"How do you know that?"

Josh shrugged his shoulders, then brushed past him. "We've talked on the phone."

What the hell? "How did you get Shea's phone number? It's an unlisted number." He should know, because he had worked to make Information give it to him time and time again. He struggled to fight off the jealousy he felt towards Josh. His partner was forming an intimacy with the woman that he wanted in his life and he hated it more than he cared to admit.

"Can't tell you that?" Josh smirked

"Don't get smug with me. I'll find my own way to get Shea's number," he promised, though he honestly thought he wouldn't be able to do it.

Craig thought back to all the times he tried to find a way to ease it out of his aunt. But she was a very clever woman and never let him have it. Asking Shea for it wasn't part of his plan. She couldn't find out how much he wanted her back then. Keeping her at a safe distance worked out better for him. Anyway, he had been too caught up in finding out the reason why his only living relative had befriended her in the first place.

"When are you going to stop acting like this is a competition between the two of us?" Josh admonished. "I hope that you know it isn't."

"Isn't that what you're making it into?" Craig demanded. "You're using Shea's hate for me to your advantage."

Josh paced around the room like he had a lot of nervous energy to burn. "Shea doesn't hate you. She cares a lot about you, but you're too thick to see what is right in front of your eyes."

Craig stood directly in front of Josh's path to make sure he got the clear cut answers he wanted. He didn't have any patience for his buddy's double talk today. Shea was avoiding him, and he had to find a way to make her open up. All this nonsense about Josh going out on a date with Shea had to end. He wouldn't let him walk Shea to her car after dark, not with the abilities he possessed at charming women out of anything.

Neither Shea nor Josh knew about the nights he stayed up late, pacing around his bedroom and thinking of ways to get Shea to not see him as the enemy. He didn't doubt he was partially to blame for placing the ideas in her head, but he couldn't tell a woman he barely knew that he had fallen in love with her.

Weeks went by before he was even able to admit to himself that his feelings for Shea bordered on something that wasn't hate. But once it settled in his mind, the realization scared the hell out of him, and that was why he always lashed out at Shea. Anytime she came within ten feet of him it was over and his hormones kicked in. When he started thinking with his cock instead of his regular head, things always tumbled downhill.

"I mean it, Josh, if you don't stay away from Shea you'll wish that you had."

The silence that hung in the air after his comment was so thick Craig almost choked on it. Deep down he knew Josh wouldn't betray him like that, but his emotions for Shea ran so hot and heavy that they clouded his judgment.

"C.C., I'm trying my best not to take your outburst personally," Josh exclaimed in a voice that held more than a trace of anger. "Have you forgotten how you would date bimbo after bimbo just to compare them to Shea? The last time you came over to my house I couldn't watch the football game because you kept talking about how Shea wasn't paying any attention to you. Even your Aunt

Rebecca got tired of the mixed signals you kept tossing at Shea. She was one of the smartest women I've ever known. She told you to stop playing games with Shea, but you didn't listen."

Craig hated when anyone pointed out his faults. *Who does Josh think he is, drilling me like this?* He knew the women he dated in the past were eye candy. If he wasn't mistaken Josh was the one who suggested that he do it with the first woman. How dare he toss those mistakes in his face now? His buddy hadn't complained about all the extra attention the women gave him back then just to get closer to the *exclusive* Craig Evans.

No one truly understood how hard it was for him because he was already born into a wealthy family. In addition, he founded one of the top graphic design companies in the state of Maine. His answering machine was always full of unwanted messages from women he didn't know and had no interest in knowing.

"Are you lost in your own thoughts again?" Josh interrupted, waving his hand in front of his face. "You've got it bad for her, don't you?"

"Stop asking me stupid questions." He smacked Josh's hand out of his face. Sometimes he wondered how he stayed friends with his partner for so many years because their personalities were so different. He was a planner and made lists to make sure everything gotten taken care of. Josh, on the other hand, jumped right in the middle of things without thinking twice about it.

"I see we have a problem here, and I'm going to help you out." Josh nodded like he had everything under control.

Craig's eyebrows furrowed "What kind of help are you offering me?"

"I'm going to make you more like me." Josh grinned as he made his way over to a leopard print chair in the corner on the room.

Being more like Josh wasn't even on his top twenty lists of things to do before he died. However, his interest was peaked. "I know I'm going to hate myself later for asking this, but what do you have in mind?"

"Take a load off and I'm going to tell you how to win the heart of one Shea Anderson."

Chapter Seven

Dear Journal,

Well, I guess that I was wrong about Craig. I haven't heard from him for about three days now. I knew I shouldn't have gotten my hopes up about him, but I couldn't help it. It's hard not to fall for a man as sexy as Craig, but I need to push him to the back of my mind and focus on all this money Rebecca left me.

What am I going to do with a lipstick company? I don't know the first thing about running a business like that. Maybe I'll order a pizza tonight and rent a good movie. I always think better on a full stomach and after a good belly laugh.

"I wonder what Craig would do if he knew you kept a diary about him," a soft but strong voice teased over her shoulder.

Groaning, Shea closed the leather bound book and shoved it back into her oversized purse, underneath her desk. "First, I'm too old for a diary," she corrected. "I've a journal, and it isn't always about Craig, for your information." She spun around and glared at her boss, Wanda Lincoln.

"Honey, don't lie to me. You know I caught you writing in that thing more than once at work. No matter how many times you call it a journal, it's a diary."

Light blue eyes sparkled with mischief as Wanda took a seat on the edge of her desk. "It's not doing you any good to lie to yourself. Craig holds most of your thoughts, and the other half is wrestling with a way not to fall more in love with him."

Falling back in her seat, Shea tilted her head to the side. "Are all those cigarettes you smoke going straight to your head? Love isn't what I feel for Craig. Hate…contempt…boredom are better words to use when you bring that man into a conversation with me. Do you know he had enough nerve to forbid me to accept a date from Josh?"

"I'm surprised Craig didn't make you swear to avoid Josh at all costs. That man has feelings for you. I don't see how you don't see it. Haven't you ever heard the old saying about how the eyes are the window to a person's soul?" Wanda tapped her new nails on her desk.

"Of course I've heard of that saying, who hasn't? But, the only thing I see in Craig's eyes when he looks at me is anger. He's upset that Rebecca left me *Luscious Lips*, and he should be. I don't know the first thing about running a million dollar company."

"You aren't going to give it back to him, are you?" Wanda scooted closer to her. "Rebecca left you that money for a reason, and you need to find out what it is."

"No, I love my job here and the pay is wonderful. I couldn't ask for a better career." She left out her dream of owning her own business. "Craig can have *Luscious Lips* and sell it to the highest bidder for all I care. I'd rather have Rebecca back. I'm counting the days down until Thanksgiving comes, anyway."

"Speaking of turkey day, what are you going to do? Are you going back home to see your folks?" Wanda asked, sliding off her desk leaving a trail of peppermint and rose body spray behind.

Shea grinned so wide that it almost split her face. "I sure am. I have a new nephew that I haven't gotten a chance to hold yet."

"I didn't know Virginia had another child."

"No, my sister didn't have a baby. My brother's girlfriend did."

Wanda's mouth opened and closed like a fish out of water before she fell down into the cushion chair at the side of her work area. "Your little brother," she whispered.

Shea nodded. "Taymar is the daddy."

"Isn't he in high school?"

"He'll be a senior next year," Shea replied, feeling Wanda's shock at her news. "My mom called me crying for a week about how her baby was too young to have a baby of his own. Then Taymar wanted to come and spend two weeks with me. I told him no and then hung up the phone."

"I don't know what to say," Wanda said.

"Wish me luck that when I go home. I won't have to stay and play referee between my parents and Taymar for the three days I have off," Shea sighed, dreading the trip.

"Sweetheart, after hearing news like that take the whole week off," Wanda suggested. "I can handle it around here without you for seven days."

"Are you sure? I don't want to put you in a bind or anything." Shea couldn't get over how generous Wanda was being. She loved her boss like a second mother, but sometimes when it came to work Wanda could be a stickler.

"Take the week to help your family and think about how you're going to win over that sexy Craig Evans. What I wouldn't give to run my fingers through all that long, thick brown hair." Wanda moaned with a gleam in her eye that showed up through her glasses. "He's one hot young man. Why couldn't I be twenty years younger?"

Shea chuckled at the way Wanda spoke her mind. Her boss was at least thirty years older than her, but acted and talked like a much younger woman. She was never at home on the weekends because she was constantly looking for new things to experience.

"You never know. Call Craig up and ask him out. He might actually say yes," Shea teased.

Standing up, Wanda pulled a pack of cigarettes from her pocket along with a lighter. "Sweetie, the only reason the mouth-watering, hazel-eyed Craig Evans would go out with me is to find out more information about you."

"Why do you keep saying that? Craig only has one interest in me," Shea denied, "and that interest is in the money and stocks from the company."

"Shea, it's time you grew up and stop living in a fantasy world. Craig has it for you bad, and everyone knows it. Hell, even Craig knows it, too, but the only thing that had kept him quiet is you. He knew you didn't see it," Wanda informed her.

"However, those days ended the second Josh made a play for you. Craig isn't going to stand for another man tasting what he considers his," her boss continued as she headed for the door. "Craig is going to make his wants known sooner than you think, so be ready. He doesn't act like a man who has been told no much in his life." Lighting her cigarette, Wanda strolled out the door, leaving a cloud of smoke behind her.

Reaching underneath the desk, Shea pulled out her favorite pastime and grabbed the black pen off her desk. Flipping open to a blank page, she let her hand started to fly across the blank pages.

I just had the craziest conversation with my boss, and I can't believe she just told me the same nonsense Josh did on the phone. Craig isn't in love with me. How could he be and I never noticed it? Yet, I did catch him a couple of times staring at me when I visited Rebecca, but I never thought anything of it.

Wait a minute! Then there was that time when he came into to kitchen and helped me with the appetizers for Rebecca's birthday party. Have I honestly been that blinded and not seen what was right in front of my face?

Closing the book for a second time that day, Shea stuck it back into her purse and reached for the stack of insurance forms in front of her. "I'm not going to believe Craig is into me until I hear it from him."

Organizing the insurance forms, Shea placed them on the stand by her computer and then started typing in the information into the correct screens. She liked her job, but this was the part that she disliked the most. Hitting the enter button, she waited while all the information saved to the correct screens and then continued working on the rest of the stack, trying to make a sizeable dent in it for tomorrow.

Hours later, Shea relaxed in her leather chair, stretched her arms above her arms, and looked around the room while she thought about where to have lunch. Yesterday she brought her lunch and the day before the Wanda had ordered it for them, so today she was on her own since Wanda had left for a business meeting.

Dropping her arms back down on the desk, she quickly shoved the remaining papers into a pile. Her eyes scanned the desktop for a large manila envelope for the completed insurance papers, but there wasn't one.

Shea twirled around in her chair and looked through the stack of envelopes on the counter behind her and still came up empty. "I know I dug some of those things out, so where are they?" She continued to search for them and she finally spotted one under a stack of new claims forms.

The office door opened and closed behind her.

"I'm about to leave for lunch. Do you mind coming back in an hour? I'll be glad to help you," she said, pulling at the end of the envelope.

"That's why I'm here. I was wondering would you like to have lunch with me," a sexy, yet familiar voice inquired, sending her system into overdrive.

Shea's heart stopped for a full second before she spun around and her gaze landed on Craig on the other side of her work area. The royal blue Polo shirt he was wearing looked sinful against his tanned skin, making her body automatically responded to his.

Today Craig hadn't brushed his hair back off his forehead, but left it loose so a lock of it fell against his forehead just the way she liked it. She did notice that the ends no longer went past his shoulders, but brushed the collar of his shirt.

Why am I getting punished like this? Shea let her gaze trail lower, over the tailored slacks down to the expensive shoes that covered Craig's feet.

The scent of expensive cologne and a self-assured man filled her weakened senses, making it hard to concentrate on anything but what it would be like if Craig finally gave her the one thing she wanted the most from him: to finally know what it would feel to have those sculptured lips pressed against hers.

"Lunch...just the two of us?" She gestured, waving her hand between the two of them. Shea shook her head and finished the job. "No, I don't think so. I like to savor my food and relax. I can't do that with you."

"Why can't you?" Craig answered, leaning down on her desk and blocking everything else from her vision but him. "I can be very relaxing when I want to be. Care to let me prove it to you?"

A flow of moisture pooled between her legs at the thought of how Craig could make her body unwind for him, and not one of them involved lunch. *Stop it now! Don't let him charm you. Craig is here for a reason and having lunch with you isn't it.*

"I don't think that a good idea."

Standing back up, Craig slid his hands into the front pockets of his slacks, pulling the material tight across the area she craved to know more intimately.

"I'm not about to take no for an answer. You were about to go to lunch, so let's go," he told her in a tone that dared her to disagree with him.

Shea thought about telling Craig to shove his ultimatum down his throat, but then changed her mind. *Why shouldn't I go? What would it hurt?* The only other time she had the opportunity to share a meal with Craig had been at Rebecca's, and then he hadn't been alone. He brought a date that had reminded her of all the women he favored — tall, slender, and size zero.

Today she was going steal a page out of Wanda's book and do something adventurous.

"Is this lunch invitation so you can drill me about the papers I need to sign?" Shea inquired, grabbing her purse. "I know where you stand about that."

"I want to drill you about my aunt's estate, but this lunch date isn't about that," Craig admitted as she walked past him. "Maybe if you're good I'll give you a hint over lunch."

Images of their sweaty bodies tangled up on the white sheets on her bed as Craig made love to her made Shea stumble in her tracks. A strong arm quickly encircled her waist and tugged back to a warm solid chest.

"Are you okay?" Craig whispered while his fingers stroked her stomach through the thin, silky top she was wearing. "I'm not used to having you fall at my feet and I don't want you to start now. Your spunk is one of the things I find attractive about you. It turns me on more than you'll ever know."

Her traitorous body shivered under Craig's playful caress as another pool of moisture gathered between her thighs. She had to get away from him or after lunch she'd have to go home and change her underwear. "I'm fine," she said, moving Craig's hand off her body ignoring the last part of his comment.

"Where do you want to eat?" Craig asked, smiling as he held the door open for her.

"I don't care as long as I can get a good meal," she answered, locking up the building.

"I've the perfect place," Craig grinned, then placed his hand in the small of her back and took her away from her job to parts unknown.

Chapter Eight

The sight of Shea leaning over his balcony with her red skirt pulled tight across her firm ass was making his cock harden inside of his pants. Craig wanted to grab it and learn how to make her scream his name until she was hoarse.

Easing away from the open doorway of the balcony, he placed their plates of food on the table. He had hoped Shea would accept his lunch invitation, so he called his chef beforehand and advised him to fix a meal for him to warm up.

When was the last time he had to prove to a woman that he was worthy of spending time with or worked this hard even to get her attention? Women had been throwing themselves at him since he was sixteen years old. If he could wrap up the way seeing Shea in his home made him feel and then sell it, he would be richer than he already was.

God, everything was going so good between the two of them. They had a pleasant conversation on the way here. Shea did freak out a little that they weren't going to a restaurant, however he calmed her down and now here they were.

I want to kiss her so bad that my body aches from it, Craig thought as he struggled not to act on his urges. Shea wouldn't want him pawing all over her this soon. Today's meal was about them getting to know each other better and nothing else. Unless, Shea gave him a sign she wanted to be kissed, then he wouldn't feel bad when he captured those amazing, pouty lips of hers.

"Are you done enjoying the view so we can eat?" he asked, coming to stand behind Shea. He couldn't get enough of the sweet smell that seemed to flow from her every pore.

"The view from your place is amazing. Wish I had something like this to look at every day," Shea said, turning around to him. Almond shaped eyes locked with his as she took a step back from him. "I didn't realize you were that close to me," she whispered.

I wish I could look into your gorgeous face every day, too, he thought as Shea searched for a way to move around his body without touching him. "My door is always open for you." He stepped back so Shea could push past him. "You're welcome to have lunch or dinner with me anytime the urge hits you."

"What has gotten into you?" Shea asked as he pulled out her chair. "You're never this nice to me. There has to be something going on."

Craig wasn't ready to let Shea know his secret yet. Hell, it was bad enough that Josh and his Aunt Rebecca guessed what it was before he did. He invited her to lunch so he could see what the future could hold for the two of them.

"You're right. I do have something going on with me, but I'm not ready to tell you about it yet," he admitted, taking his seat across from Shea. "So, how about we eat this wonderful meal and you can tell me more about yourself." He smiled and waved his hand towards her plate. "Come on, let your guard down with me. I don't want you this distant with me."

"How did you know tuna pasta was one of my favorite meals?" Sienna eyes held his as Shea waited for his answer.

"I remember my Aunt Rebecca had it every time you came over for dinner," he acknowledged staring at Shea as she shoved a forkful into her waiting mouth.

"I'm shocked you even noticed I was in the room with the way your dates were always hanging on your every word," she said before taking another bite of her food.

Shea's jealous! The thought thrilled him because if she paid attention the women he brought around, that meant she had some kind of feelings for him.

Craig decided to eat something before he told Shea how he really felt about her. All the times he caught her at Rebecca's made his week go by better, but the times he missed her he counted the hours until he saw her again. God, it was hard for him to have this attraction to Shea on one hand and be mad at the same time.

He only wished *Luscious Lips* hadn't been left to her in the will...things could be such more different now. They could be in a committed relationship. Furthermore, Shea might actually be in love with him by now instead of wondering about his motives.

"Are you going to tell me more about your life or not?" Craig asked, then took another bite of the savory pasta. He would have to thank his chef again for making such a delicious lunch.

"What do you want to know about me?" Shea hedged.

"Do you have any siblings?" *Talk to me. I want to learn all I can about you.*

"Yes, I've an older sister and a younger brother who's still in high school." Shea replied, shoving her empty plate to the side. "You're the only child, aren't you?"

"Yeah, but Josh is like the brother I never had, so I have never felt like an only child since I met him." Craig answered, placing his empty plate on top of Shea's. "We have been friends for as long as I can remember. I tease him a lot, but he's a good guy."

"Josh can be very charming and flattering when he wants to be." Shea sighed, then smiled.

Anger raced through Craig's body as he snatched up their plates. "Follow me, we can have dessert in the kitchen," he directed as he left the table. Why in the hell did Shea think he would want to hear about all of Josh's wonderful qualities?

Inside the kitchen he fixed two bowls of coconut ice cream, placing one in front of Shea and taking the other one. "I thought Josh mentioned something about the two of you going out on a date. How did it go?"

"You already knew about my date with Josh, because you came to my job. Don't you remember that you forbade me to accept it?" She licked the ice cream off the spoon.

Craig's fingers squeezed his spoon so hard at the glimpse of Shea's pink tongue that he bent it. He quickly tossed it in the trash can, then grabbed another one out of the drawer. "Would you rather sit down? We don't have to stand up against the counter."

"No, I like this. It brings back good memories of my childhood."

"Did you eat ice cream a lot in the kitchen when you were younger?" Craig was pleased that Shea was sharing a part of her past with him. His first date with her was turning out a lot better than he could have dreamt. This was the first step in earning Shea's trust and eventually her love.

"Every Wednesday night was ice cream night at my house," Shea answered, finishing off the last of her dessert. "We would move from the dining room into the kitchen and talk about anything and everything."

"Sounds like you had a wonderful childhood," he murmured, a little envious now that he was an only child. "Hearing you talk about your big family makes me wish I had some siblings."

Rolling her eyes at him, Shea laid her ice cream bowl in the sink behind him. He tried not to groan when her breast accidentally brushed the side of his arm.

"God, I wished I was an only child almost three hundred days out of the year," she sighed. "My older sister is way too bossy and my little brother was a holy terror when we were growing up."

Stepping back, Shea folded her arms underneath her perky breasts. "I'll never forget the time when we were upstairs playing in the bathroom. I had to be about eight years old and Taymar pushed Virginia down into the tub. Luckily, she only got a bump on the back of her head and didn't need stitches."

Craig placed his empty bowl next to Shea's in the sink. He would have loved to seen how Shea looked as a little girl. He would bet anything she was full of spunk just as she was now.

"What did you do when this happened?" He caught a whiff of her unique scent and the sexy aroma made his cock harden even more.

"Of course, I ran downstairs and got my mama. She didn't play when it came to rough housing inside. I knew Daddy wouldn't have gotten on Taymar like her." Shea laughed, causing the side of her eyes to crinkle, making her even hotter.

"Did Taymar get in a lot of trouble?"

"Yes, he was grounded for two weeks and had to come straight home from school. No football or soccer practice for him, and he hated that."

Craig watched how Shea's sienna eyes lit up when she spoke about her family. He could see how much she loved them. "You're really close to your siblings, aren't you? Are your parents still alive?"

"Yes and they're about to celebrate their forty-fifth wedding anniversary," Shea answered, taking a peek at her watch. "I hope I can find someone to spend the rest of my life with. It's so rare now to find your soul mate."

Babe, you're done looking, because I'm right here in front of you, Craig thought. "I noticed you glancing at your watch. Does that mean my time with you is about over?"

"Yes, I need to get back to work and finish typing in those forms. Thanks for a nice lunch. I didn't think I would have such a good time with you," Shea replied, going past him back into the other room.

Do it now! "How about we continue this good time tonight and you let me take you out to dinner?" Craig asked.

Perplexed eyes looked up at his as Shea paused in his doorway. It was almost like she didn't trust him. "Craig, what is going on? First you ask me out to lunch and now you want to have dinner with me? I'm not sure about all of this attention I'm getting from you. Are you trying to butter me up or something?"

Bracing his hand on the doorjamb, Craig leaned down into Shea's personal space. "What are the usual reasons that a man invites a gorgeous woman out to dinner? I want to get to know you better."

* * * *

Shea didn't know if it was their proximity or the seductive smell of Craig's expensive aftershave that made the words erupt from her throat. "What time do you want to pick me up?" She wouldn't second guess her decision until she went home. Now she only wanted to live in the moment.

Winking at her, Craig took a small step back from her throbbing body, "Wonderful...let me drop you back off at work, and then how about I'll pick you up at your house around seven o'clock?"

Shea scooted back from Craig's perfect physique until she was standing outside on the front porch where the warm afternoon breeze trickled her bare arms. *How is it possible for one man to have everything going on for him*? Looks, brains, and a body to die for.

She desperately needed to ease the trance Craig placed on her body every time he came within twenty feet of her.

"I'll give you directions to my place when I get back to work."

"No need. I already know," he whispered, closing the gap she purposely placed between them, and planted a quick kiss on her mouth before she could move.

Fireworks, sparks...all her nerve endings raced through her body as her mind worked overtime to come to grips with Craig kissing her. She thought of herself as a strong woman, but something about this man turned her to mush.

"Why did you stop?" Shea said softly as Craig stepped back.

"We better go before I do something that you aren't ready for," Craig answered, closing and locking the door before he led her to his car.

Shea was still too caught up in the memory of Craig's lips moving across hers to utter a word of protest, so she just followed him to the car and secretly hoped a repeat of the kiss would happen tonight on their date.

Chapter Nine

Dear Journal,

After two years of wanting, dreaming, and wishing, my ultimate fantasy came true today. I don't know if I even have the strength to write it down. Okay, I can do this. Craig kissed me. Now, it wasn't like the kind of kiss that would make you forget your mother's name, but there were sparks and it was still good.

However, that is only part of the icing on the cake. Craig asked me out to dinner. I don't want to be excited, but I am. It's hard not to be after having a crush on him since I laid eyes on him. Can I really still have a crush on a male at my age? Is it something else that I don't want to admit to yet?

I swear I won't go over my head tonight, because I'm not quite sure of what's going on in his mind. But I do plan on having a damn good time with a very handsome man. I might even get the chance to brush a lock of that tempting hair off his forehead.

By the way, I think this is the most I've ever written in you, and you better get ready I might have another entry before the night is over. Wish me luck!

Shea snapped her black leather journal shut and shoved it under the pillow on her bed. Standing up, she smoothed the form fitting silver dress back down over her hips. After Craig dropped her back off at work, she entered the last of the insurance papers into the computer in record time and went shopping for a new dress.

"I finally have a date with Craig. I pray he doesn't ruin it by bring up Rebecca's estate. Hold up…what if Craig isn't the one that ruins the date? I could be the one that blows it."

Confidence.

Yes, that was the one trait she could use a tad bit more of in her life, to be more secure of herself as a woman and her ability to seduce Craig. The more self-assured she came off with him on their date, the harder it would be for him to resist her.

"I can do this and I will do this," Shea encouraged herself with one last pep talk. Picking up her matching purse off the bed, she checked her appearance one last time and left the room. In the back of her mind, she hoped this would be the first of many dates she would have with Craig.

Chapter Ten

"What in the hell are you doing here? Did you follow me?" Craig snapped his gaze at the person seated across from him. "I thought I told you I didn't need your help."

"I couldn't resist following you here. All day long you've had this look on your face," Josh teased. "You looked like a man in love."

"I'm not in love with Shea," Craig denied, wishing Josh wasn't so damn observant, "and stop implying that I am."

"What do you call it when a man spends most of his time daydreaming about a woman instead of working on the biggest graphic design account we have?" Josh countered in the smug way he was beginning to hate.

"Curiosity," he responded hurriedly, wanting to shut up the man in front of him. "You know I've been attracted to Shea for a while now."

"Attraction...is that what the old timers are calling it now?" Josh chuckled. "I thought it was a case of Cupid's arrow straight through the heart."

Craig's mind was feverishly working overtime to find a way to get rid of Josh before Shea arrived. He was still uncomfortable with the fact that at the last minute she refused to let him pick her up. Shea acted like it would be a strain on him to drive to her house. If she was thinking like that, then he had a long road ahead of him before Shea saw him the way he desired.

"Don't call me an old timer again. I'm not that much older than you."

"Two years is a lot," Josh taunted, waving two fingers in front of his face. "I'm only thirty-six, so I'm a youngster compared to you."

"Keep it up and see if I help you work on anymore book covers," he threatened, then grinned when his words hit their mark.

The arrogant grin vanished from his buddy's face as he jumped up from his seat, almost knocking it over in the progress. "I got to go. See you later." Josh bolted from away from the table so fast Craig swore a cloud of smoke appeared behind him.

Reclining back in his seat, Craig observed how several of the lurking women in the restaurant kept glancing in his direction. He wasn't the type of guy who frequented bars to find a woman, but Byrd's Bar and Grill served the best hot wings with honey mustard sauce in town. He couldn't think of a better place to bring Shea out of her shell. It was a neutral, yet fun place to have a second date.

Shea came off shy and uncertain around him when they weren't having a fight. However, when they argued she was full of spunk and womanly passion. He only had to find a way to bring that hidden part out of her more so he could work it to his advantage.

For as long as Craig could remember people had called him an assertive person, the kind of man who wanted to make his mark on the world.

Sure, what man didn't want to be self-reliant and strong when it came to taking care of things, but he could also be very loyal and protective when the right woman came along.

Is Shea the woman who'll bring those qualities out in me, his mind questioned as he glanced down at his watch. Where was his date? It was half past seven and she wasn't anywhere in sight.

"I know she didn't stand me up." Craig raised his hand and signaled a waiter to his table. As the waiter approached him, he spotted Shea in the entranceway of the restaurant, looking captivating in a shimmering sliver dress. He rattled off his drink order and the waiter rushed away, then he focused on his date.

Every man's head swung around to stare at Shea as she strolled towards his table, looking like a goddess. Standing up, he pulled out a chair for her, breathing in the light scent of peaches. "You look absolute stunning. I see why you were running a little late," he whispered by her ear barely getting control of his emotions. The need to kiss the back of her neck called to him.

"Thank you," Shea answered as she took her seat.

Craig wondered if Shea wore that precise scent to lure him deeper into her web of seduction. In reality, all she had to do was wiggle her little finger and he would be a goner.

"I'm not above giving a compliment when I think one is needed," he answered going around the table retaking his seat. Picking up his napkin, he laid it back across his lap. "Did you have a hard time finding the place?"

"No, there was an accident about three blocks from here and I got caught up in the traffic."

"Was anyone hurt?"

Shea shook her head, "I think it was only a fender bender."

"Good…so, have I told you how beautiful you look tonight? That dress looks like it was made for your body." *Did that sound like a line?* He hated when he heard other guys used them and now he was doing it.

"Yes, you have, but I don't mind hearing it again." Shea grinned placing her napkin in her lap.

Craig moved back as the waiter returned with his drink and set it on the table in front of him. "Do you want something to drink, a white wine or something?"

"Water will be fine," she told the waiter before looking back at him.

"Do you not drink?"

"No, I like a glass of wine every now and then, but I rarely drink when I'm the one driving home," she answered, then picked up the menu. "I've heard about this place but never had the chance to dine here. Thanks so much for the invitation."

"I've a confession to make." Craig took a sip of his rum and Coke.

Shea sat up in her seat, tossing her menu back down on the table. "Oh, I can't wait to hear it. You don't look like a man who keeps secrets."

"What kind of man do I look like?"

The sounds of chatting customers and waiters clearing off the tables faded into the background as Craig waited for Shea to answer his question. Finally, maybe now he would get some insight into how she felt about him. If it was bad he would change her attitude and if her thoughts were favorable he would only make it better.

The beginning of a smile tipped the corners of the perfect mouth he dreamt about kissing while he was sitting behind his desk at work. He needed another test run to make sure it was a soft as satin.

"No, I'm going to keep it to myself until I know you better," she said softly.

"Why won't you tell me now? In the past at my aunt's house you never had a problem telling me what you thought," Craig stated, staring at Shea. "Sometimes you talked so much I thought your mouth ran on batteries."

Shea's smile faded a little when he looked at her, and he could almost see her reverting back into her shell. He couldn't let that happen. "Don't sit there and let me be rude to you. Tell me what you're thinking."

"It won't do any good. You'll turn into the Craig who finds a way to criticize me," Shea blurted, scarcely aware of her own voice. "I don't know how I even thought we could enjoy two meals in a row with each other." Pitching her napkin down on the table, she stood up.

Craig cursed under his breath as he shot out and latched onto Shea's arm. "Don't leave. I've had a long day and Josh has been getting on my bad side. I'm sorry if you didn't take my comment as a joke, because that's how I meant it."

"I'm still not sure if this is a good idea, but I'll stay." Shea took his hand off her arm and sat back down. "We don't have that much in common to keep a conversation going."

Oh, I'll find something for us to talk about. "How about I'll give you some more insight into me since we discussed your family at lunch," Craig suggested satisfied by the fact that Shea hadn't left him.

"Are you going to tell me what we have in common with each other? So, after you're finished, what am I supposed to see? Will you be the ying to my yang?" she teased, smiling at him.

"I might just say we go together like peanut butter and jelly," Craig tossed back. He loved this lighter side of Shea. She almost came across like she was more comfortable with him.

"You don't seem like a guy who would eat peanut butter," Shea said, eyeing his body.

"Why not?" He frowned. "I love the crunchy. I eat it right out of the jar with a spoon. It's a weakness I can't resist."

"You have one of the hottest bodies that I have ever seen on a guy."

A rush of jealousy hit him full force in the middle of the chest at the thought of Shea staring at another man's body that wasn't his. How many guys had she given this same compliment to already?

Whose body was better than his? He looked damn good for a guy who was about to hit forty.

He was dying to ask Shea how many men she had slept with, but it was none of his business. Craig struggled to maintain an even, conciliatory tone when he asked his next question. "How many guys have you told that in your life? Gorgeous as you are, I'm sure you've had plenty of boyfriends, maybe even a few fiancées?"

The mischievous look in Shea's dark, haunting eyes made him wish he had bitten his tongue. "I thought we were going to discuss you instead of me. How am I going to see if you are worth spending my time with?"

Craig was impressed with confidence he heard in Shea's voice. She seldom acted this away around him, and it was turning him on. He wanted to spend some alone time with her, away from all of these people. "How about we leave here and I'll take you somewhere else to eat?" All the prying eyes at the restaurant weren't what he wanted tonight with her.

"Am I going to like this new place?"

"I think you might. I usually go there when I need to clear my head about things," he hesitated, and then measured Shea for a moment or two. Maybe he should let her know where they are going instead of springing it on her. "Do you want me to tell you before you make a decision?" Something flickered in the back of Shea's eyes, but he couldn't put his finger on what it was. "No, I don't. Tonight is my night to be more spontaneous and I'm going to do it."

More spontaneous. Craig bit the inside of his mouth to keep from asking how far Shea was willing to go. "Let me pay for my drink and we can get out of here. I'll drive you there and then we can come back and get your car." He waved the same waiter back over to the table and asked for the check.

"No, I rather follow you in mine and save that extra trip back here," Shea insisted. "I like having my own transportation when I go out on dates at night."

Craig tossed a few bills and a tip inside the black folder the waiter left on the table then got up. "You're a smart woman. We better hit the road. I still need to feed you, so I hope you don't mind eating a home cooked meal again."

Walking around the table, he pulled out Shea's chair for her and then placed his hand on the small of her back. He felt so proud escorting her through the crowded place. He smiled at the men who tossed him envious looks. *Yeah, she's with me and there's nothing you can do about it.*

In the cool night air, with the moonlight highlighting them, Craig made sure that Shea was secure and buckled inside her cute white Nissan before he got behind the wheel of his silver Jaguar. It was the first big thing he bought when he landed his first huge account for *Evans Graphics.*

He had been so lost in getting his business off the ground that he didn't miss the company of a good woman until Shea Anderson appeared in his life. Now he only wished he had more ways to show her what he would do for her if she opened up more to him.

"Don't worry, Evans, you haven't lost an account, and you aren't about to let Shea slip through your fingers, either," Craig promised himself as he started his car and drove out the parking lot with Shea following closely behind him.

Chapter Eleven

The night air blew through the open window, tickling the ends of her hair against her cheek. Reaching up, Shea brushed her hair back with the tips of her fingers, then rested them back on the steering wheel. What was she thinking, agreeing to go with Craig to some place she didn't know about? Had she lost her morals and common sense?

Deep set, hazel green eyes, perfect brown hair, and a permanent five o'clock shadow shouldn't have this effect on her. She wasn't a young girl anymore, but she had a crush on Craig like she was still in middle school and he was the unattainable football star.

She slowed down as Craig turned down a memorable street that entered her life and stayed a part of it for over two years. Why were they here? Was Craig trying to prove a point about something?

Pulling in behind Craig, Shea turned off her car and sat inside fuming until Craig got out of his and came over to her. She swallowed hard, trying not to reveal her anger but failed. "Why are we here? Is this some sort of joke?" she yelled at Craig through the open window.

"No, it isn't a joke and I'm not playing a game on you. I've been coming to my aunt's house a lot lately.

I didn't have the heart to sell it after she died. So I kept it and turned it into a getaway place. Josh doesn't even know I still have it. Will you please come and let me fix us something?"

Craig looked at her with such a passionate expression that all the anger left her body. Rebecca was her friend, but she had been Craig's aunt and he was still mourning her death. Her flash of anger moments before yielded to compassion for the man she cared about and shouldn't. "Okay, I'll come in with you."

Craig opened her car door and then helped her out. "Thank for agreeing to stay with me. I loved my parents, but I was very close to my aunt. Anytime something was bothering me I could come to her."

"Rebecca was like that. She helped me through a tough time in my life about a month before she died," she confessed, waiting for Craig to unlock the front door.

"What did she help you with?"

She gave Craig a searching look, and then walked into the house past him, surprised by how Rebecca's presence and love still surrounded her. "I was thinking about packing up and moving back home to help out with my father with his business. He didn't think my brother was mature enough to handle a baby, go to school, and work for him all the same time. I still can't believe my little brother is a father. It's so strange."

Craig closed the door behind her, cocooning her in wonderful and cherished memories. "I'm glad my aunt talked you into staying here."

"I'm surprised you cared either way since you always saw me as the enemy," Shea said. "I think you always saw me as your enemy."

"I've never saw you as the enemy," Craig corrected, moving to stand in front of her. "I was jealous by the fact Rebecca showered the same amount on attention on you as she did me. I didn't want to share her with you or anyone else."

Shea was having a hard time understanding why Craig hadn't been close to either one of his parents. Did they abandon him as kid on Rebecca or something?

"Can I ask you a personal question? You don't have to answer if you don't want to."

"Sure, ask away." Craig led her over to a sitting area by the front window. He waited until she sat down, then, took a seat. "What has gotten your mind all filled with unanswered questions?"

"You were so close to Rebecca and I've never heard you talk about your mother and father. Did the three of you not get along?"

Dark brow eyebrows shot up in surprise at her question. "No, my parents were wonderful people, but my Aunt Rebecca was fun and loved to joke around. I wouldn't go on family vacations with my parents to spend time with her. We would play catch or football in her backyard. I appreciated her laugh. It was so carefree and she never let anything bother her.

"My parents worried a lot about how to keep making more and more money so my aunt took *Luscious Lips* away from them and they hated her for that. They tried to get it back several times but they failed. On my eighteenth birthday she promised to sign over the company to me when I turned forty."

"Why forty? Why didn't she just give it to you on your birthday?"

"Rebecca didn't believe in giving people things without them working for it. Anyways, she knew my dream wasn't to run a cosmetics empire. I loved art way too much, so she told me to follow my heart and apply for graphic arts school.

"In the back of my mind, I never doubted the company would be mine until you befriended her and Rebecca gave all the stocks to you."

Nervously she moistened her dry lips. "You hate that, don't you?"

* * * *

What good would it do to deny the truth? "I'm like my parents on that part of the business. I want it stay within the family."

"I saw that quality in her the second she walked through the door at my job," Shea mused. "I'm really going to miss her, but you don't have to worry, I won't keep the stocks. I'll sign them over to you on Thanksgiving."

Hearing that Shea was going to let him have his family business pleased him, but he still had other ideas planned for the two of them. She just wasn't aware of it. When he got through with her, Shea wouldn't be the same woman.

"I'm a horrible host," Craig complained, getting up from his seat. "I invited you here with the offer of a good meal and I'm not fixing it. How about we make our way into the kitchen and I'll see what I can throw together?" He stuck out his hand and waited for Shea to take it.

"I don't know if I can eat another one of your wonderful meals. I might not be able to drive myself back home afterwards."

"You're more than welcome to spend the night here. I promise that I won't seduce you in my aunt's house. I'll wait until I get you back at mine before that happens." He grinned, and then winked at an astonished Shea.

"What am I supposed to say to that?" she gasped.

"Nothing," he retorted. *Oh. Yeah.* His plan was working way better than he thought it would.

Chapter Twelve

Lying down on the bed, Shea reached under her pillow and grabbed her journal, kicking off her heels to get more comfortable. She was still in a state of bliss over how perfect her second date with Craig had turned out. They didn't kill each over dinner or when they decided to play a game of pool.

Dear Journal,

Let me see if I can describe my second date with Craig in one word — Unbelievable!!!! I can't believe he's the same guy who got into an argument with me outside the lawyer's office at the elevator. Tonight he was funny, sweet, and very charming. If I didn't know better I would think he had a twin or maybe a clone. He shared a part of himself with me tonight, making me understand more why Rebecca meant so much to him.

After we finished having dinner at Rebecca's, Craig took me back into the living room and showed me pictures of him as a kid inside of an old photo album before we headed downstairs. Even back then he was a heartbreaker.

Oh, these words aren't portraying all the fun I had tonight with him and nothing will. A part of me is still back on the date wishing it hadn't ended. I'm a working woman and I had to leave Craig there. However, a small part of me is wondering if he is still thinking about me.

* * * *

Back at his house, Craig moved away from the window when he saw his guest getting out of his car and strolling up the driveway. He didn't want to seem overly anxious, so he waited for the doorbell to ring before opening the door.

"Mr. Terry, I want to thank you for coming by so late. I know my house isn't on your way home," Craig said, shaking hands with the older man.

"You know I shouldn't be here like this without Miss Anderson with us."

"I know, but this won't take long. I only have a few questions that I want to ask you about my aunt's will," he replied, shutting the door then showing Mr. Terry to his seat.

"What is it exactly that you need to know, Craig?"

"I've a question for you. What if something happens and Shea doesn't sign over the property to me by Thanksgiving?"

"The property will become hers. All she has to do is sign the paperwork in my office with me as the witness."

Leaning forward, Craig rested his elbows on his thighs. "I thought the property went to her automatically. I didn't know she had to sign papers to make it official. Does Shea know about this, too?"

He paused while Mr. Terry adjusted his wire rimmed glasses and scratched the top of his balding head. Neil had been his aunt's lawyer as far back as he could remember, and was a very fair and honest man. "No, I'm going to tell her about this tomorrow after my court case."

"Why don't you let me do it?" he offered. "Her office is on my way to work and I wouldn't mind making a quick stop at all, it does involve me, too."

Mr. Terry's eyes narrowed suspiciously. "Not a good idea after the way the two of you acted in my office."

"We are on speaking terms now."

"Sure you are," Neil laughed, pushing up his glasses. "Shea hates you and the feeling is returned tenfold by you."

"I don't hate her. I'm going to toss something your way that might surprise you."

"As long as I have been a lawyer, Craig, there isn't anything you can tell me that I'll be surprised by."

"Get ready to fall out of your seat..." Craig paused. "Shea and I have been on two dates since that meeting in your office."

Mr. Terry stared at him speechless for a full minute, and then erupted, "What kind of game are you playing with Miss Anderson? She's a nice, caring young woman, not your type at all."

"How do you know what my type is?" Craig snapped, incensed that his aunt's lawyer presumed to know about his love life.

"I've seen you all over town with several different women and none of them looked like Shea."

"You mean black?"

"No, I mean without an ulterior motive or in awe of the famous graphic designer. Pick which one that you want to believe, but Shea will never fall into either category."

Craig wasn't fond of how this conversation was turning out. Was there something going on he should know about? "Neil, do you have a soft spot in your heart for Shea like my aunt did? Aren't you my family's lawyer? Which means you should be on my side?" He hated how some men couldn't get past a pretty face. Shea was a very attractive woman with her caramel skin and huge, chestnut eyes. Nevertheless, he knew something deeper was going on in that head of hers.

"C.C., I was Rebecca's attorney, and I'm here to make sure her final wishes are carried out," Mr. Terry corrected in a harsh tone. "I've been married for almost forty-two years. Miss Anderson is young enough to be my daughter. I don't like what you are implying."

Common sense told him to stop pushing the subject but he couldn't. "You aren't going to tell me anything else, are you?"

"Rebecca told me what a smart young man you were." Mr. Terry got from his seat and the air in the room grew cooler with each passing second. "Now, I advise you to leave Shea and this will signing alone. Let her make her own decision about it. Any manipulations on your part might come back and blow up in your face."

Craig hadn't asked for a lecture and he wasn't pleased that Mr. Terry thought that he could give him one. Free advice or not, it was uncalled for. "I'm really tired from the long day I've had. I'm sure you wouldn't mind showing yourself out."

"You're playing with a woman's emotions, and if you aren't careful it's going to come back to haunt you," Neil warned before he left, closing the front door with a loud snap.

"I guess that I'm on his bad side now, but I've all the right in the world to ask about my family's business," Craig complained. Standing up, he left the room for his work area on the other side of the house. He still had to finish the graphics on a book cover and the deadline was tomorrow.

* * * *

"Is there a Shea Anderson working today?

Shea's gaze darted from the computer screen and landed on a huge arrangement of flowers positioned in front of her face. They looked and smelled wonderful, totally taking her by surprise.

"I'm her."

"Here you go, ma'am," the delivery girl grinned, handing her the glass vase. "You must have some guy really into you. I can't even get my husband to buy me a rose on my birthday."

"Wait, let me give you a tip." Shea sat the flowers on the desk and reached down for her purse.

"It's already been taking care of at the flower shop," the girl said, giving the boutique a longing look before she spun around and left the office.

Shea stared at the huge arrangement and then reached for the card. Big, bold masculine print marked the center of the purple card.

Are you free tonight?

Craig

485-2897

Should she call him? Their last two dates were flawless. She would have guessed Craig was such a gentleman, but tonight she already had plans and they couldn't be cancelled.

Everything was moving so fast between the two of them, and her mind needed time to figure things out. Only one person could help her with that. Tapping the card against her chin, Shea closed her eyes and tried to think of a way to let Craig down easy.

"Maybe I should have sent you roses if the current bouquet is putting you to sleep," a deep timbered voice teased from the doorway.

Shea jumped up in her seat and her mouth dropped open at the sight of Craig slouched in the doorway with a hunter green shirt unbuttoned, showing off the light dusting of hair of his chest. Since Wanda was still on vacation she decided to work in her office. The position of the office made it harder to hear when the front door opened.

"You look very handsome," she commented, getting up from her seat. Shea took a few seconds to stick the card back into the flowers. "That shirt really brings out the small flecks of green in your eyes."

"Shea, my eyes aren't green." Craig laughed, coming into her workplace closing the door behind him.

Men, she thought, easing around her desk. "No, when you get excited these little specks of green pop out in your eyes. I noticed them last night when you talked about your business. I found it very sexy."

"You think I'm sexy?" Craig questioned, arching one eyebrow.

"Are you fishing for a compliment, Mr. Evans? I don't know if I should give you one or not."

"I'll make it worth your while if you do," he whispered, wrapping his hands around her waist.

The hotness of Craig's hands made Shea step closer to him and rest her palms in the middle of his solid chest. "On a scale of one to ten I'll give you about nine and a half."

"Why am I not a ten?"

Cocking her head to the side, Shea eyed Craig's rugged features with feminine pleasure. He was a perfect ten, but she shouldn't let him know that just yet. "Now I can't let you get a swelled head, can I?"

"Babe, I've had a swollen head since I walked into the room and saw you in that red shirt," Craig breathed, rubbing his lower body against hers.

The thickness of his erection burned her through her off white slacks, and the thought of Craig inside of her made a sudden pool of dampness between her thighs. "I've been thinking about ways to get you out of it tonight after dinner," Craig confessed before his mouth covered hers hungrily.

His lips were hard and searching as his tongue parted her mouth and stroked the roof, causing tiny shivers throughout her entire her body. Never in her life had a man stolen all her senses with just a touch. Draping her arms around Craig's corded neck, she tried to deepen the kiss but he raised his mouth.

Brushing the corner of her mouth with his thumb, he gazed into her eyes, "I can't get into this with you. I'll be late for my meeting. Hell, if I didn't have that late lunch date I'd spend the next hour showing you how much I wanted this kiss not to end. Can we pick this up at dinner tonight?"

"I can't have dinner with you tonight."

Leaning back in her arms, Craig frowned down at her, "Do you have a date or something? I thought we could have a romantic dinner, rent a horrible movie, and have a make-out session in my living room. We could pretend like we're horny teenagers."

"I'm sorry, but I can't tonight. I've other plans. I'm meeting a friend for dinner."

"Anyone I know?" Craig asked, rubbing her back. "Maybe I could tag along and then after dinner we could still go back to my place for a movie?"

"Sorry, I can't." Shea answered, stepping back. She wasn't about to let Craig come in here and sweep her off her feet after only two dates. He had more work to do than that.

"Man or woman?"

"What?"

"Is your date with a man or a woman?" he demanded.

"I don't have to tell you that." Shea moved away from Craig and sat back down. "We aren't involved with each other. We only had two dates with each other. I can have dinner with whomever I want."

Bracing his hands on her desk, Craig took over her personal space as he leaned across it. "Do you want me to find a way to get the answer from you? I think I can find a way to make you talk pretty quickly. I can still taste you on my mouth and I wouldn't mind seconds." He smiled at her, all traces of his anger from earlier gone. "Do you think I can have another taste?"

"We don't have time for this conversation." Shea found it impossible not to return his charming smile. "It's time for you to go."

"I want to go with you. I might be able to provide some comic relief if your date gets too boring."

Shea shared another smile with Craig before she said. "I don't think so." She was surprised that he would even suggest such a thing. "I'm sorry, but I can't have dinner with you tonight."

"So, you are going out with a man?" Craig accused like she hadn't said a word to him.

Shea barely hid her smirk in time. Craig was covetous at the thought of her going out with other men. They had only been on two dates and he was already acting like a jealous boyfriend. "Why should I tell you that? We aren't in a relationship with each other." *Not yet at least*, she thought. "Are you going to answer my question?" she asked before taking another sniff of the sweet smelling flowers on her desk.

"Are you going to answer mine?" Craig countered.

The anger in Craig's voice didn't escape Shea, and her grin finally broke through. "I think the green-eyed monster is taking over and I'm flattered."

Craig gave his head a quick shake, causing the familiar lock to fall onto his forehead. "I don't get jealous. We're friends, and I'm only concerned about who you go out with. You're going to be a very wealthy lady pretty soon and I don't want some lowlife taking advantage of you."

Friends? Craig only saw her as his friend and nothing more. She wasn't expecting that word to come out of his mouth after the kiss they just shared. Shea hastily placed a blank expression on her face and then answered him, so he could get out of her sight.

"I'm glad we're friends." She almost choked on the word. "I won't forget about your concern, either, but you don't have to worry about my date tonight. I hate to be rude, but do you mind leaving? I need to finish all this paperwork." Shea waved her hand towards the stack of insurance forms in front of her.

Frowning at her sudden change in demeanor, Craig came around the desk and confronted her. She saw the confusion in his spectacular eyes. "You totally just did a one-eighty on me," he pointed out. "What did I do to cause this sudden change?"

"Absolutely nothing," she lied. "Don't you have a lunch that you're going to be late for?"

Craig slowly dragged his gaze away from her face down to his watch. "Shit, I've fifteen minutes to get across town. I don't want to leave without knowing what I said to cause that sad look on your face."

Shea forced a fake smile as she tried to hold herself together. "I already told you that you didn't do a thing to me. Craig, I really need to get back to work, so you have to leave or I won't get out of here on time."

A doubtful look filtered across Craig's face as he stepped away from her. "You're lying to me and we both know it, but I don't have the time to go into this. However, I'll catch up with you later on and you'll tell me the truth." He promised before he left her alone in the office.

Shea waited until she was sure Craig was gone before she pulled her journal out of her top drawer.

Dear Journal,

Let me tell you what happened today. Craig sent me some flowers with a card asking me out on a date. I thought we were moving forward at a wonderful pace. I was beginning to think we might have something, and then he stopped by my job and called us just 'friends.'

Can you believe that? I was totally off on this one. Thanksgiving can't come quick enough for me, so I can sign those papers and get him out of my life. Well, I can't let it bother me. I still have the dinner tonight with Pierre and hopefully it will be good news.

Chapter Thirteen

"I thought this news would bring a smile to your face. Haven't you wanted this for a while?"

Taking a sip of her Cosmopolitan, Shea placed it back on the table as the sound of club music played in the background around her. "Pierre, you know I'm excited, but I'm still about three thousand dollars short."

Pierre Thomas, her friend and real estate agent, laid her dark sable hand on top of hers as a sign of comfort. "Honey, you'll be able to get it if you use money Rebecca left you. You're rolling in money now. I don't understand why you won't touch it."

"I didn't make that money from *Luscious Lips* and I don't want any handouts. All those stocks belong to Craig and I'm going to sign them over to him." She glanced away from the look Pierre gave her and continued. "You know I've always been a person who wanted to make my own success. I think that why I was so attracted to Craig. I saw the same qualities in him."

Pierre puckered her mouth. "I thought you were half in love with him."

Good Lord, she didn't want to repeat the words Craig told her this afternoon, but the more she said them the better they would sink in. "He only thinks of us as friends."

Shea not only heard Pierre's sudden gasp but felt it, too, and the look of pity in her friend's eyes about did her in. Pierre had a soft spot for happily ever after and thought every woman had her own Prince Charming waiting for them.

"Are you sure you didn't misunderstand him?"

"No, he said it very clearly."

"Well, forget about him. There are so many other hot guys out here that could be your soul mate in hiding. I know all of them would love the chance to date a hot, intelligent future business owner like yourself."

"How can you always be so positive?" Shea sighed while her fingers played with the stem of her glass. "Don't you ever have a down day?"

"Pierre Thomas never has a bad day. I'm always in a pretty good mood. You would be, too, if you went after what you wanted and stopped being so damn shy."

She had never thought of herself as a shy person. Sure, maybe she was a little reserved or withdrawn sometimes, but never shy. "I'm not a shy person and you know that," she admonished.

With a wave of her hand Pierre dismissed her. "Fine, you aren't shy but you would never approach any of these guys in here tonight, and you know I'm telling the truth."

Pierre always had the uncanny ability to read her and she hated it. "You don't work the extra hours I do at the insurance agency. I need to save up so I can open my own bed and breakfast. That takes up most of my time and a man can't fit into my life. It's now totally focused on *All the Fixin'*.

"Is that what you're going to name it?"

"Yes," she replied.

"Very cute. The name reminds me of a good home cooked southern meal," Pierre sighed. "However, you did have time for a man and his name was Craig Clark Evans. I have to confess, I'd skip work for a while to be with him, too. A woman could get lost in those eyes of his.

"I remember when I sold him that building for his graphic art business. He smelled so damn good. Shea, don't let him get away from you." Pierre practically purred as she relived her memory of Craig, and Shea was torn between laughing at her crazy friend and telling her to shut up.

Sometimes Pierre didn't want to listen or believe the things she told her. Or, it went it one ear and right out the other. "Did you just not hear what I said? Craig only sees us as friends."

"Haven't you ever heard that the best lovers are usually friends?" Pierre mused, wiggling her eyebrows.

Shea couldn't help but laugh at her friend's silliness. "What am I going to do with you?" Pierre's attitude constantly put a smile on her face no matter what the situation was. She was overjoyed to have a friend like her in her life.

"How about you buy me another drink and then I'll find us a couple of hot guys to dance with?"

Men of all race, shapes, and ages filled the local hot spot as Shea stole glance around the room. She wasn't really interested in meaningless chit-chat with some stranger, but Pierre was right: a quick dance wouldn't hurt. Her wandering gaze finally spotted a man over in the far right corner that reminded her of Craig. "All right to the drinks and the dance if you pick that guy over there," she agreed, staring over Pierre's shoulder at her potential dance partner.

Spinning around in her seat, Pierre ogled the guy she wanted. "He isn't the perfect Craig, but I see why you picked him. Okay, order my drink and I'll get you a dance with him." Pierre got up from the table, then got into her diva mode as she sauntered over to the man in the corner.

"Lord, please don't let that guy think Pierre and I are two of the craziest women in the world," Shea said out loud as she looked around for a waitress so she could order more drinks.

Chapter Fourteen

"How could you tell Shea you only thought of her as a friend?" Josh drilled. "I thought you were trying to build something with her."

"I am trying to build something with her, or I was until she told me she had another date," Craig replied as he ran down the track past the pond with Josh. "I got jealous and blurted out the friends thing."

"Did she get upset or quiet like most women do with stuff like that? I know I've lost a couple of girlfriends tossing the friends word around."

Seasoned joggers zipped past them while Craig thought about how Shea backed away from him at her office. He almost skipped his appointment to make her understand that he hadn't meant it like it came out. He definitely wanted more from her than just *plain old* friendship.

"Shea told me to leave because she had to finish working. She never told me who she was having dinner with." He ran past a woman with a baby stroller and thoughts of having a family with Shea crossed his mind. "I called her until midnight, but she never answered her phone."

"Come on, let's stop and talk." Josh ran off the track and fell down on the grass, and Craig followed him.

"Do you think she spent the night with some guy?"

"Nope, I can't see that happening. It doesn't seem like something Shea would do. She's the kind of woman every guy wants to bring home to his mother. I've always thought of her as the all-American girl," Josh added.

"Yeah, but with a sensational body, a killer smile and a personality to match," Craig said, wiping the sweat from his brow with the palm of his hand. "I think I might have messed things up big time."

"Man, don't get down on yourself yet. You only need to find a way to get back on Shea's good side. How about flowers, candy, or a stuffed animal? Women love that stuff."

Craig was skeptical that Shea wouldn't shut him out even further. He had tried to apologize but she wasn't listening to him yesterday at her office. If he stayed any longer she might have gotten out of her seat and shoved him out the door. His stupid comment landed him feet first on the bad side of Shea, and he didn't know if he had enough charm or skill to get back on good terms with her.

"You weren't there. You didn't seem the look on her face and hear the disappointment in her voice. It's going to take more than the things you described for me to reconnect with her."

What had he done? When was he going to learn to think before he opened his big ass mouth? Shea let him be himself and he loved that quality about her. There wasn't an ounce of pretense in her entire body. He had been looking forward to digging beneath the surface and finding out about her hopes and dreams.

"Have you tried calling her today?" Josh asked, turning his head to look at him.

"Josh, I've left three messages for her and she isn't returning them."

"Maybe she's busy. Didn't you tell me her boss is still out of town? Shea is a working woman and her job will always come first."

Craig liked how Josh was trying to smooth over the damage he had done from his friends slip, but Shea was avoiding him and both of them knew it. "Thanks for that, but she's mad at me and I have to find a way to fix it. I don't want us to be just friends. I've never wanted that kind of bond with her."

Josh stared at him, then looked away out at the pond a several feet in front of them. "Do you honestly have feelings for Shea now or are you still trying to find a way to get your company away from her? You did make me cancel my date with her."

"You shouldn't have asked her out when you knew I was interested in her," Craig hissed then quickly got his temper back under control. "How I feel about Shea now has nothing to do with getting *Luscious Lips* back. Please don't confuse one with the other."

Standing up, Josh brushed the grass off the back of his shorts. "I need to get back home and get ready for my date with Tina. I met her at the health club yesterday and she's sizzling hot."

"What are you going to do when you miss out on your future wife by dating all of these gym groupies?"

"How about you focus on finding a way to get Shea back in your life and not about my dating habits? When I'm ready to settle down you'll know it, and so will she." Josh waved at him, and then ran back down the track in the direction they came from.

Once Josh's voice finally left his head, Craig let his mind wander back to all the fun he had with Shea when they weren't at each other's throats. He never experienced that much pleasure on a date before without sex being involved. She wasn't helpless and didn't need his help at every turn. A small part of him had been disappointed at how capable she seemed of handling every situation she was in.

Shea would never be able to keep anything from him, because one look at her face and he knew what she was thinking. It had only been twenty-four hours and he was already missing her terribly. It was like a caffeine addict going through withdrawals. Nevertheless, he had no intentions of giving up his addiction. Shea had to talk to him and he wasn't giving up until he made it happen.

Getting off the grass, Craig brushed off the back of his running shorts, and as he turned to leave a flash of red by the pond caught his attention. *Shea!* He couldn't believe his good luck.

"I'm not allowing her to leave until she hears me out," Craig swore as he hurried towards the other end of the park. She should have known that he wasn't going to let her blow him off like that.

* * * *

"Are you sure I only have a month to make another bid on the place? I thought I had at least eight more weeks to come up with half. Pierre, you know I can't come up with that amount. I'm not going to lose that house. You've to help me think of something."

Sitting on the bench, Shea cradled the phone against her shoulder and pulled out the bag of breadcrumbs for the ducks from her purse. "Can't you hold them off for me? I'll have the money by the end of January. Wanda promised me a raise and with the money I already have saved it that should be enough."

"Honey, these buyers are serious about the spot. They want it for a miniature golf course, however you might get lucky. The other buyers are going overseas for two months to close down their other business. They're going to make a bid for the property when they get back, and if I'm right they should return around the first week of January."

"Can you lose their paperwork until then, and that will give me extra time to get all the money. I want that spot. It took me over two years to find it and I've worked long hours to save up for it. I only need a little more time."

Shea heard Pierre's deep sigh in her ear, and that meant things weren't looking good for her. "I can't make you any promises, but I'll show them two more places that are closer to town. Maybe one of them will catch their eye," Pierre replied. "But I'm going to be honest with you, this corporation really adored that area you have your heart set on."

"Just do what you can." Shea knew she was fighting a losing battle, but she wasn't ready to give up just quite yet.

"Okay, I'll talk to you later, Shea."

"Thanks, Pierre, and I'll call you back tonight."

"I won't be home until at least eight o'clock," Pierre said. "Bye, Shea."

"I'll call you then, bye, Pierre," Shea hung up the phone and flung it into her purse.

Opening the bag of crumbs, Shea pitched several handfuls to the greedy ducks that surrounded her feet looking for a free, fattening meal. She envied how they didn't have a care in the world. She longed for her life to be as simple. For the first time, she wondered why she couldn't have been born lucky, or at least wealthy.

"Is Pierre the man you dumped me for yesterday?" a rough-edged, strong male voice demanded behind her, causing her heart to jump up in her throat. "Why didn't you tell me about him when I brought it up?" "With us just being friends you don't have any claim on me," Shea replied above the pounding of her heart. She couldn't look back at Craig or she'd get lost in those impious eyes she loved staring into so much.

"I need to talk to you about that." Coming around the bench, Craig scared away the ducks as he stood in front of her.

Her mouth went slack then dry at the sight of Craig's sweat-covered chest and rippled abs blocking her view. A pair of black trunks molded his hairy, muscular thighs and her gaze went up to the impressive bulge nested between his slightly spread legs.

Shea shook her head, trying to dislodge the dark fantasies that enticing sight brought to her mind. She tried making make eye contact with Craig, but caught him staring at her breasts. Why was he looking at her like that when he only wanted them to be friends? It pissed her off. She was good enough for a few stolen kisses here and there or a lustful look, but not good enough to be Craig's girlfriend. What in the hell was his deal?

"I didn't know you jogged here. This is my first time seeing you here," she retorted a little harder than she intended.

"I don't. Josh jogs here three times a week and he dragged me along for company today," Craig answered, giving her breasts another hungry ogle and joining her on the bench.
"How long have you been coming here to feed the ducks?"

"For a while now. Rebecca introduced me to it and I found it relaxing, so I kept coming after she passed away." Shea tossed the ducks another handful of crumbs.

Sliding his left hand behind her, Craig reached inside the bag with his other hand and threw the ducks some bread. After he was finished he turned his attention completely on her, his penetrating gaze raking up and down her body slowly like he was stripping away all of her clothes.

Shea became nervous and a little uneasy under Craig's scrutiny. She stirred around on the bench trying to get more comfortable and to block out the sensations of what his look was doing to her. She was supposed to be mad at him, not still lusting after his fine ass.

"Are you planning to sit there and look at me all day?"

"I couldn't imagine a more beautiful sight to look at," he said, running his calloused fingers hand down the side of her arm, "but I do want to talk to you about something."

"What is it?" She shuddered as Craig's index finger played with the bow tied at the end of her short-sleeved shirt.

"I want to apologize for what I told you back at your office about seeing you only as a friend. I lied." The words were spoken low but with a power behind them.

Mixed feelings surged through her at Craig's apology, but how was she supposed to answer him? He only admitted that he didn't see the two of them as friends, but he never said he saw them as a couple either.

He's trying to sweet talk you, her mind warned. *Remember this one word when it comes to Craig...Playboy.*

"Don't you want to know how I see us?" He eased his hand from her sleeve to the bows on the front of her shirt. "Do you want to know if I got jealous at the image of you going out with Pierre instead of me? How about if I got drunk last night when I couldn't get hold of you?"

A warm glow flowed through her as she fought to control her raging emotions. Shea couldn't help herself "Will you be honest if I said yes?"

"Of course," Craig leaned over and ran his tongue down the side of her neck. "You taste like strawberries."

Heat like she never knew before captured any words she may have spoken and sent all her withheld desire rushing through her body to parts that hadn't been explored in years. Craig was trying to seduce her and, as much as she wanted to, she couldn't fight it.

Moving back, Craig placed his finger under her chin, making her stare into his eyes. Her body ached for his touch and the burning flames she saw returned in his glance startled her.

"I want us to date each other and no one else. I've feelings for you and I want to explore them. You're the type of woman I've been waiting for a while now. Do you want to see how far things can do between us?"

She was unnerved by the sudden change in Craig. Her stomach twisted up in knots at the thought of all of this being a lie to get the stocks away for her. She couldn't deal with Craig's seduction along with her money problems. He was such a complex man and it was hard to get under his thick skin. What if he was only allowing her a peek to eventually break her heart?

"I'm not sure about this. We are so different on so many points."

A determined look burrowed into his forehead as Craig slid closer to her. "Haven't you heard that opposites attract?"

"We are definitely opposites," Shea agreed, "but what I'm worried about is if there will be an attraction after the sexual one fades away. You don't seem like a man who would stick around waiting for me to make up my mind."

"I wouldn't mind waiting for you, so will you give me another chance? I don't want us to be friends. I want to be your lover, protector, and in the end something more." Craig linked her fingers with his and kissed her knuckles. "However, being a friend is fine, but I won't be the kind of that listens to you talk about your dates with other men."

"Oh, you want to be a friend with benefits?" Shea questioned, tugging at her hand. She should have known Craig wasn't serious about this.

Tightening his hand around hers, Craig tried to make stop her freeing movements, but she got loose anyway. "No, I want to be the man you fall in love with."

Shea looked at Craig with surprise, recalling his hostility only weeks earlier at the reading of Rebecca's will. He couldn't stand her...no, he detested her. Now he wanted her to fall in love with him? She stood up, shocked and more confused than ever. "I don't understand what you're doing to me. One minute we're going out to dinner, then you're calling me your friend and now you want me to fall in love with you."

"I'm tired fighting what I feel for you," Craig confessed, pulling her back down to the bench. "I want you and I need you in my life. Can you at least tell me I have a fighting chance over the Pierre guy? I know I'm better for you than he is."

She was caught off guard by the sudden urgency of his voice. Craig actually sounded like he cared about her, but that wasn't possible. They barely knew each other. They had a long way to go before she could tell him she was in love with him, even if she already was.

Shea shook off Craig's grip and shoved the bag of bread crumbs back into her purse. "I can't commit myself to this, Craig. You might be playing some kind of game with me. Can't we go back to having dinner with each other and work from there? Falling in love with you wasn't a thought in my mind, because you never acted liked you wanted a steady girlfriend."

Craig tilted his head and there was a slight hesitation in his brown eyes. "Did you sleep with Pierre? Is that why you don't feel I have a chance at winning your heart? Or did my indifference push you into the arms of another man? My aunt always warned me about my quick mouth and temper."

While her mind was spinning with bewilderment from Craig's confession, Shea got up from the bench. *Why do men think when a woman turns them down another man is involved?* Craig would be so embarrassed once he found out who Pierre was. Her friend constantly got mistaken for a man because of her name.

"Not that it's any of your business, but I haven't slept with Pierre because we don't have that kind of relationship."

"Good...I'm glad you told me that. Now, what time do I pick you up for our date?" Craig got up from the bench. He towered over her while his fingers wreaked havoc with her body by touching the side of her neck. "Do you know how my times I daydreamed about your silky hair spread across the pillows on my bed?"

"Stop saying things like that to me, or I won't be able to go back to work," Shea scolded, taking a step back from Craig. He had a way of making her want to live out her secret desires. She wanted to yield to the blazing liquid fire that seemed buried within her. "I can't have dinner with you tonight. I've other plans."

"With Pierre."

"Craig, I've got to go, but I'll call you tonight and we can set up another time to have dinner." Standing on her tiptoes, Shea brushed her mouth across his firm lips and stepped back before he could take over the kiss. "Don't think I don't want to discuss this further because I do, but I can't right now."

She blocked out the passion she felt radiating from his body and spun away, hurrying back to her car. She couldn't get sidetracked by Craig tonight. not when she needed to talk to Pierre.

* * * *

Picking up a pebble off the ground, Craig flung it into the pond and watched as it skipped across the water. He wasn't going to let Shea have a date with another man tonight. When he was coming towards her earlier, he saw her smile while she talked to the guy on the phone. He wanted to put the same look of elation on her face. His body had been asleep until Shea waltzed into his life, and now his breath caught every time she looked at him.

Shea's strength, passion, and determination made him want to protect and love her, but she acted like that thought scared her. She seemed to be a little leery of his attentions and that pained him. He was a complex man, not easy to know on a personal level or intimately, unless he decided to let somebody in.

"Shea, you better get ready. You thought I was tough before, you haven't seen anything yet," Craig swore as he left the park.

Chapter Fifteen

"Don't leave me hanging. Do you or don't you have good news for me?" Shea asked as soon as the door closed behind her. "I had to leave work early because I was making myself sick thinking about it.

"Hello to you, too, and I had a wonderful day at work. Thank you for asking," Pierre replied, placing her purse and briefcase down on the couch. "I sold two houses and a third one might be in the works. The potential buyer is going to call me back tomorrow."

Shea was thankful for her darker skin so Pierre wouldn't see what was certainly her face turning red from embarrassment. "I'm sorry. I know that you've got other things to do besides keep my house safe from other buyers."

"Don't worry about it." Pierre sighed and picked a grape off the tray on the living room table and popped it into her mouth. "I have bad news and good news for you," she said around the food in her mouth. "Which do you want first?"

"Of course the bad news," Shea exclaimed, worried

"The developer hated the other houses that I showed him and still wants to place a bid on your house."

94

Her world started to crumble around her the second the words left Pierre's mouth. "You couldn't stop this at all?" she groaned.

Pierre flopped down on her couch, then proceeded to kick off her three-inch heels, "Honey, didn't I tell you that I had good news to go along with that bad news?"

She started to perk up some at the delighted expression in Pierre's smoky eyes. "Yes, you do. So spit it out. What's the good news?"

"The miniature golf company can't make an official bid on that certain house until the first week of February. They still need to settle another real estate matter first, that I told you about."

Rushing across the room, Shea jumped down on the couch and almost knocked Pierre off. "Does that mean I still have enough time to make an official bid without them breathing down my neck?"

"That's what I'm saying, but you need to do it ASAP because once they bid you won't be able to outbid them. The owner wants the house gone and will take the first bid offered."

Some of the joy bubbling inside her body faded away, and was replaced with a deep fear. "How can you be sure someone else won't come along and take it away from me? I'm still short on money."

"Am I a good friend to you? Aren't I here to help you through difficult times?" Pierre asked with a dazzling smile.

Shea forced herself to settle down and not panic. "Yes, you have been an outstanding friend over the past five years. I don't know how I made it without you."

"Don't get sassy with me, missy, or I won't tell you my secret." Pierre reached for a cheese puff on the serving tray. "And I know you'll want to hear it."

"I apologize. I'm just worried I won't get my dream house after it took me years to find it. Go on and tell me your secret."

Pierre ate two cheese puffs, and then got more comfortable on the couch, purposely trying to drive Shea crazy with waiting. "You'll be the only bidder on the house because I happened to accidentally misplace the papers to show the house today. Now, if my boss finds out about this I'm going to be out of a job, but you'll have time to get the money saved up."

Screaming at the top of her lungs, Shea wrapped her arms around Pierre. A sense of strength came over her as she realized her long-awaited dream might come true. Her mother took her to her first B&B when she was a little girl and every year after that until she turned eighteen. It was always their little getaway while her brother and father went fishing and hunting.

"How can I ever repay you for doing this for me?"

"I always want a room to be available for me whenever I call," Pierre replied, "with breakfast in bed and a single hot hunk in the room next to mine."

Laughing at her friend, Shea hit Pierre on the shoulder, then got up from the couch "If I get my B&B I'll try my best to do that." Turning, she headed for the kitchen with Pierre complaining behind her.

* * * *

"C.C., this isn't a good idea. How about we go back to my place? I can order two large pizzas with everything, and I've got a case of beer in the refrigerator," Josh suggested as he got out of the car behind him.

"No, Shea didn't want to have dinner with me. I only want to get a look at the competition." Craig was standing on Shea's doorstep. He looked down at his clothes, straightened them, then rung the doorbell. "I'm not leaving until I get a chance to see this guy in action."

"This is going to bite you in the ass."

"Stop being my dictator and be my friend instead. I would be there for you if you needed help with a woman," Craig growled as he heard footsteps coming towards the door.

* * * *

"Were you expecting someone beside me?" Pierre asked, glancing over her shoulder towards the front door.

"No, I didn't invite anyone else to dinner besides you," Shea said as she made her way to the door. Well, we are about to find out who it is," she said, opening the door. Shea stepped back as Craig and Josh walked into the house without being invited. "What are you doing here?"

"I came to see this guy you're so fond of," Craig said in a harsh voice. "He must be pretty special to blow off a date with me."

Shea slammed the door and then moved to stand in front of the overly sexy, but angry man who just invaded her house with his favorite sidekick. "I'm not having dinner with another man."

"Hey, you're dating another man and didn't tell me about it?" Pierre chimed in behind her. "I thought we were friends. You're supposed to tell me everything."

"Pierre, be quiet so I can straighten things out with Craig. I'm upset he showed up unannounced at my house like this."

Craig stared at her and then stared Pierre on the couch then directed his gaze at her. "Pierre is a woman? Why didn't you tell me this?"

How dare he jump on her like this! "Because it wasn't any of your business, and you didn't give me a chance to. You were too busy talking at me to listen to anything coming out of my mouth." She crossed her arms under her breasts and tried to disregard the thrill it gave her that Craig was jealous. He was such an ever-changing mystery to her.

"Okay, maybe I did get a little out of hand, but you weren't being honest with me, either."

Shea opened her mouth then snapped it shut, stunned by Craig's bluntness. How could he toss her being dishonest in her face? He was constantly switching between hot and cold when it came to him. If anyone was being dishonest, it was him.

"Will one of you say you're sorry so I can go home?" Josh complained. "I still have enough time to order a pizza before the basketball game starts, but I've got to leave in the next five minutes."

Shea determined that this wasn't the time or place to drag Josh or Pierre into her fight with Craig. They could discuss this when they were alone and without prying eyes. She had to be the better person and apologize first. "Craig, I shouldn't have let you think I went out on a date with another guy."

Stepping inside her personal space, Craig traced the side of her jaw with his finger. "No, honey, I was the one who was wrong. I had no right to demand anything from you when I still haven't proven I want us to be exclusive."

"Great! The two of you are all crazy for each other again," Pierre sighed, making Shea swallow down a smile. "Now I can leave, too. I have to go over the floor plans for the house I'm supposed to walk through tomorrow."

"Don't leave, Pierre," Shea said. "You and Josh can stay and we all can watch the game together. We can make a party of it."

"I don't think Craig wants that," Josh told her. "He wants to spend some alone time with you. I've never seen him have it so bad for a woman."

Craig brushed his mouth over her lips, "He's right you know," he breathed low enough for only her ears. "The two of them should leave. We can do something with them another time."

"I agree with Josh," Pierre giggled, getting up as she slipped around Craig's large body. "I really should get home and feed Spike, too. The last time I was late that crazy dog didn't come around me for two days. He went through his doggy door and stayed in the backyard."

"Shame on you," Shea scolded, moving back from Craig. She was annoyed at him for tempting her like this with people around. He loved making her all hot and uncomfortable without any way to relieve it. "Well, if I can't make you stay at least let me walk the two of you to the door."

Leaving Craig standing to the side, Shea escorted Josh and Pierre to the door. "Remember, I want the two of you to come back another time so we can all do something together," she said. "Our best friends should know each other better since Craig and I are together at the moment."

"I'll try to do my best, but you know this is the hottest time in the market for me. If I can get away I will," Pierre promised, then kissed her on the cheek before going out the door.

"Same here with me," Josh said, then followed Pierre into the night air.

"We are going to be a couple for a long time, Miss Anderson," Craig whispered, coming up behind her. Closing the door softly, he pulled her back against his chest, wrapping his arms around her waist.

"Are you sure about that?" Shea taunted.

"Positive," he growled, kissing the side of her neck. "You're stuck with me."

"Even if I don't sign over your aunt's shares to you in a couple of weeks?" she edged.

Craig's grip tightened for a second on her waist, then loosened. "You have the right to do anything you want with those. I'm not here to pressure you into anything. How about we don't talk about that?"

"Okay, so what do you want to talk about instead?" she asked, spinning around in his arms.

Shea noticed how Craig seemed relieved to be released from the conversation, but she didn't voice her concerns. Craig wasn't the type to hide things he was too much of an in-your-face guy. Besides, Pierre had given her some wonderful advice, Rebecca had left her those stocks for a reason, and maybe the bed and breakfast was the best way to invest it.

Chapter Sixteen

"How about we discuss ways I should punish you for making me jealous of Pierre? All I could think about on the drive here was finding you with another man."

"Craig, you're out of your mind," Shea teased, kissing him on the side of the mouth. "You know the truth now, so let's drop it."

"Why are women like that?" Craig asked. He pulled Shea's shirt out of her jeans and traced the small of her back with his fingers. "They can get jealous of their man being with a girl they don't know. However, they never like it when a guy gets jealous and questions them."

"What, are you putting me into a group?" she asked, pressing her breasts to his chest and placing her arms around his neck. "I'm my own person."

The feel of her hard nipples almost made Craig lose his train of thought. He was growing tired of the light touches and the tempting kisses here and there. He was more than ready to make love to the warm bundle in his arms. Removing his hands from her waist, Craig reached up and took the clip out of Shea's hair. Raven hair brushed her shoulders and he glared at the new length.

"When did you cut your hair?" He loved Shea's hair the other way because it gave her a sweet look. This new style made her look like the sexy siren he knew she was.

"This afternoon, it was getting to be a problem for me. I was going to cut it shorter but decided not to."

"It looks good. How about we make our way over to the couch and I can show you without words how much I love it?" he suggested, dropping his hands down and squeezing Shea's tight ass.

"You're a very naughty boy," she groaned, wiggling her lower body against his throbbing cock. "Oh, seems like you're more than ready to show me."

Blood pumped through his veins and his pulse rate shot up as he thought about becoming one with Shea. His mouth went dry at her suggestion, he had dreamt for months about being with her that away. He had wanted Shea even before he knew her name, but he sensed she wasn't quite ready for him

"Are you ready for this?' Craig questioned. "Do you want us to become lovers?"

Her gaze caressed his face as Shea's small hands teased the ends of his hair. His erection grew thicker and harder.

"How can you ask me something like that? I've wanted you ever since I saw you standing at the edge of Rebecca's pool."

His throbbing body shuddered at the memory of Shea pulling her hourglass figure out of the pool. She captured him then and never knew it. "But, as much as I want you, I don't want our first time to be like this." He couldn't do that to her, no matter how much his body demanded a release.

"Like what?" She leaned back from him.

"In the heat of the moment, because I want it to be romantic a night neither of us will forget." It was vital that he cherished her in way no other man had or ever would. She was his woman, and he had to show her how much she meant to him, with and without words.

"I didn't know you had this romantic side to you. You come across so brass and arrogant. I'm touched," Shea confessed softly.

Being romantic had never been a part of his makeup. Sure, he could be a gentleman, but he wanted to go further with Shea. Make her understand how extraordinary and rare she was to him. Maybe even bring out that wild side that she kept hidden away like a buried treasure.

"You make me want to do things I've never done before. Like wake up in the middle of the night and watch you sleep. Learn little cute things about you, like if you sleep on your back or side. How about if you snore or don't snore?"

"Shit, I wouldn't care if you did," Craig admitted. He wasn't used to telling a woman his feelings like this, but with Shea it was like second nature. She made his deepest wishes a reality.

"Darling, you need to stop talking like that before I forget you turned me down," Shea exclaimed, giving him one last kiss. "Now, what can we do to kill some time and burn off all this extra energy?"

Picking Shea up by the waist, Craig carried her over to the couch He covered her body, with his loving how the contours molded perfectly to him. "I gave us a rain check to be cashed in later by me," he corrected.

"Why do you get to cash it in?" Shea pouted, drawing his full attention to her plump bottom lip. "What if you're looking too damn sexy one day and I can't wait to have my way with you? Do I really have to wait for you to make the first move?"

Male pride and arousal surged through Craig as he stared down at the woman he knew someday would be his wife. It was only a matter of making her believe in him and the relationship he was trying to build for the two of them.

"Honey, anytime you want to have your way with me I'm game." He loved this new, adventurous side of Shea.

Switching their bodies around, Craig pressed Shea's back to his chest. This was the life that he had always wished for but never thought was possible. He was falling in love with the knockout wrapped in his arms. Words he never thought about before were starting to roll around in his head: *Provider, protector,* and *father*.

Kissing the back of Shea's head, he tightened his arms more securely around her waist. "Babe, what are you thinking about so hard? You're awful quiet. Want to share your deepest thoughts with me?"

Shea linked his fingers with hers then rested them on her stomach. "You honestly want to know?" she asked.

Yes, tell me. I want to know everything that goes on in that brilliant head of yours." The more he learned, the better leverage he had to win her over.

"I was wondering about your past girlfriends and how long you stayed with them. It seemed like every time you came to Rebecca's house there was a different woman on your arm."

I bet you have more on your mind than that. "The women you saw me with never lasted more than two weeks tops. Turned out after a couple of dates we didn't have much in common." *Come on, ask me your real question.*

He heard Shea take a deep breath before she continued, "Have you only always dated those types?"

We're getting closer.

"What types are you referring to?" Craig replied like he didn't already know the answer. Tossing his leg over Shea's thighs, he placed them into their own paradise with his body heat as the warmth.

"Waif-like models with long hair, big doe eyes," she said, rattling off the qualities of his past four girlfriends.

She isn't going to ask me, he thought, disappointed. "Shea, stop stalling and ask me the question that you want to know. You're dying to know if I've ever dated a black woman before."

"Have you?"

"Yes, back when I was in college, but it ended and not on good terms." He prayed his honesty wouldn't open more questions that he would have to answer. It happened years ago and he liked for his past to stay in the past.

"What happened with...?" Shea paused, waiting for him to fill in the name.

"Olivia. I started dating her freshman year," he answered.

"Why did you break up with her?"

Craig shifted his weight on the couch, nervous about answering Shea's question. He didn't want to admit the truth and change her opinion of him. Not when she was finally starting to see him in a different light. It wouldn't look good that the only interracial relationship he had ended badly. "I dated Olivia years ago. Why are you so interested in what happened?"

"Every woman wants to know how her man's relationships ended with his ex-girlfriends. It gives her a glimpse into her future with him." Shea twisted around in his arms until they were face to face. "I can sense you're hiding something from me. Did you do something to her? Or was it her? It can't be that bad unless she caught you cheating on her," she teased with a smile, then tapped his chin with her fingertip.

The smile vanished for her face when he took too long to answer her question, "You cheated on her," she gasped moving back from him and getting off the couch.

Chapter Seventeen

"Shea, stop. Don't let a relationship from my past ruin what we are trying to build together," Craig begged, tugging her struggling body back to his. He knew he should have kept his mouth shut. He was having a hard enough time making her believe that his attentions were honest.

"You haven't had the best of luck with any of the women from your past. I won't be the next name marked out in your little black book." She knocked his hand off her arm. "I want us to work on something that is going to be long-term. I'm not talking about marriage, but how do I know the only thing you feel for me isn't infatuation?"

He was determined to straighten out the frustration Shea was experiencing. She couldn't possibly think he had placed her in the same category as his past relationships. He would prove that she meant more to him. "Go away with me this weekend?"

Craig was surprised by the words that left his mouth, but he didn't care. Reaching out, he stroked Shea's cheek with his fingertips and was surprised by how cold her skin was. What brought that on? Was she frightened to be alone with him somewhere new? Did she think he was going to hurt her?

"You're so cold. What's wrong?"

"Nothing," she murmured, moving her head away from his touch.

"Yes, there is something going on, and I want to know what it is," he exclaimed, worried about what was going on inside of Shea's head.

"How can you think about us going away with each other when I'm concerned about what direction our future is headed in?" Shea said, hurt. "Do you only want to have sex with me, and that's why you suggested the weekend getaway?"

Frustrated that he couldn't get Shea to see he was being honest, he said, "No, honey, I want more than sex from you. I want us to have a deeper more meaningful connection than that," he confessed, "It took me a while to realize why I fought so hard to stay away from you. I would still be fighting how I felt if Josh hadn't pointed it out to me. I want us to have some time away from here so we can just focus on each other. Not on Aunt Rebecca's will or the deadline that Mr. Terry gave to us. I think we both need a place to call our own for the next five days. Can you get the time off or is Wanda still out of town?"

* * * *

Don't you dare mess this up by overanalyzing it!

Shea saw the pleading look Craig was fighting hard to keep from her. He did want this time with her as much as she did. If she went away with him, she knew it would change their commitment to each other. There was no way they wouldn't make love to each other the second the door closed behind them. The heat between them almost burned her alive.

The way he lightly caressed her skin made her realize Craig knew how a woman wanted to be touched, and she wouldn't be disappointed with him like the other men from her past. She couldn't let his or her past ex's prevent her from exploring what could be something electric between the two of them.

It seemed like he had gotten over the whole will thing and wouldn't care if she kept the money and used it toward her bed and breakfast. Now, he didn't know about the B&B yet, and this weekend getaway might be the perfect time for her to drop a few hints and see where it would lead.

Craig was an amazing businessman and might give her a few tips on how to acquire a better business plan. She loved working with Wanda, but she hadn't planned on staying at the insurance firm forever.

A trip away would give her time to dig further into her subconscious about how much of her heart she wanted to give Craig. He already had so much of it without knowing, but was she willingly to give that last bit to a man who had the ability to crush it in the palm of his hand?

Stop worrying and go for it.

"Yes, I can go away with you. Wanda called me from home before Pierre came over. She wouldn't care if I took some of my vacation time early. Most of the work that needs to be done in the computer can wait until I come back."

Warm, hazel eyes shined with pleasure as Craig leaned down and captured her mouth for a quick wet kiss. "You don't know how happy I am to hear you say yes. I've the perfect place for us to go."

Licking her lips, Shea could still taste Craig on her mouth and she loved it. "Are you going to tell me?" She would go anywhere with this man.

Rich, masculine laughter filled the room as Craig ran his thumb over her bottom lip. "Woman, can't you let a man surprise you? You always want to ruin the surprise."

"Will it be good?" she asked, and they both knew she wasn't talking about the surprise.

"I know it will be something that you'll never forget."

"I've had men tell me that before and it was forgettable," she countered.

Shea didn't miss the flash of jealousy that crossed Craig's handsome face and it made her smile. It was good to know that he could get that away about her.

"Those other men won't even be a memory after me, and that's a promise," he growled passionately.

"You sure are confident of your abilities," she teased. "How do I know this isn't all just talk?"

Craig rested his weight on his elbows and stared into her eyes. "We don't have to wait until our trip. I'm still ready and able to prove just how good I am. The question is, are you ready for me?" His gaze dropped down and raked over her body like he was envisioning her naked.

Heat like she had never known before engulfed her, making her body involuntarily lift towards his, "No, I think we should still wait until we leave," she whispered, trying to control her urge to kiss Craig's mouth. Craig had his body at an angle where she could feel the warmth, but it was just far enough away that his chest wasn't touching hers.

God, had her nipples ever felt this hard before? She struggled not to rub them against Craig to stop the aching sensation. Would one little touch be so bad?

"Shea, you look like you're in pain. Is there anything I can do to help you?" Craig breathed as he stroked the side of her neck with his fingers.

"No, I'm fine," she gasped as a moist tongue came out and replaced his fingers. He had moved a few inches, but still not enough for her to feel his chest. That devil knew he was driving her body crazy and he was enjoying it, too.

"Honey, are you sure?" he asked between licking and sucking the side of her neck, sending tiny shock waves of desire throughout her limbs. "I'm here to please you and I don't mind helping you relax before I leave."

Answer him, her mind thought, but words were the last thing on her mind. She wanted Craig to move his mouth to where it could be put to better use. "I'm sure," she lied, trying to block out her need.

"I don't think you're telling me the truth," Craig denied, lifting his body away from her.

"Why do you say that?" Shea asked, staring him directly in the eyes as the scent of pure male made her mouth go dry.

"This," he said as his thumb and index finger toyed with her enlarged left nipple poking through her thin shirt.

"Oh my God," she screamed as her nails dug into the couch cushion. "You've got to stop I won't be able to take it." Her nipples were the most sensitive part of her body. Craig couldn't keep playing with them or she would go crazy.

"I think I might have hit the jackpot," Craig grinned as he quickly sat up and lifted her body so she straddled his thick thighs. "Can I take a look at my prize?"

Pulling her bottom lip between her two front teeth, Shea gave Craig a quick nod before he unbuttoned her shirt and pushed it to the side, then waited as he made fast work of her bra. She waited in silence as his eyes stared at her breasts. Did he think she was more than a handful? Why wasn't he saying anything to her? As one of her old insecurities resurfaced, Craig took her left nipple in his hot mouth and sucked.

Some tangible bond joined Shea to Craig as his hand came up and massaged her right breast. The feel of him working both her breasts made her purr in the very back of her throat. She felt her pulse leap with excitement as his mouth shifted to her other breast and his hand dropped away.

"Shea, you taste so good, like chocolate icing on top of a warm piece of cake," Craig whispered lifting his mouth from her chest.

She tingled as his hands pushed up her skirt and he rocked his cock to her wet center, but she had to keep her wits about her. "Oh, you're making it so hard for me to send you home," Shea panted, skimming her hands over Craig's wide chest.

"Then invite me to stay," he suggested, pressing his hardness against her letting her feel how it swell even more. "I'm more than ready to please you for the rest of the night and early into the morning."

A delicious tremble of want raced through her as her bad girl side pushed to get it; however, it slapped her back down. "I can't do this with you, at least, not yet," she apologized. "I'm not prepared for this, are you?" His nearness was overwhelming, and she almost changed her mind until Craig raised her off his body, placing on the couch next to him.

"No, I didn't bring any protection with me, either," he sighed, dejected.

* * * *

Craig relaxed on the couch while Shea fixed her clothes and then pulled her hair back into a crooked ponytail. He hated that he hadn't gotten the opportunity to make love to her yet. It wouldn't be so bad if fantasies of being wrapped in her smooth arms weren't controlling his every thought. Now something else happened preventing them from making love.

"C.C, don't worry about not having any condoms. I'll make sure we'll have plenty of them next time," Shea promised, getting up from her seat as she walked behind him.

Spinning around on the cushioned seat, Craig gawked at Shea. "What did you call me?" Hearing his nickname coming out of her mouth made the hairs on the back of his neck stand up.

"C.C.," Shea replied, looking at him like he had grown a second head. "Do you have a problem with that?"

Craig loved that Shea felt comfortable enough with him to call him by his nickname. Hopefully this meant that she was coming around to see the two of them as a couple. He wondered what other things he could get her to agree to if he worked at it long enough. The possibilities were endless, because something new and exciting was bound to happen on their trip, and he couldn't wait.

"No, I liked that you called me C.C., but I love how my birth name sounds coming from your lips. Your voice adds a raspy quality. It gives me a pleasure like I've never felt before."

"I don't mind calling you anything you want," she confessed, easing closer to him. "How about if I call you darling or sweetheart?"

Coming back around the couch, Shea's hand reached out to touch him again, but he moved back before she made contact. He couldn't let her touch him, because his body still hadn't cooled down all the way yet from their earlier foreplay.

"Shea, honey....please don't." Craig begged, leaning away. Shea truly had no clue what she was doing to him.

A frown marred her smooth forehead as she stepped away from him. He not only felt, but saw the heat that radiated from her body. "Is there a reason you don't want my hands on your body?" Shea crossed her arms over her chest, making her body language speak volumes without her even knowing it.

Latching his hand around her slim wrist, he tugged her closer and unhooked her arms. He laid her left palm over his pounding heart. "Don't go reading things into my comment that isn't there. My control is slipping more and more each day when it comes to you. I'm trying to fight the urge to make love to you right now, but I don't know if I'll be able to keep my hands to myself on our trip."

His gut clenched tighter when Shea's tongue darted over her top lip. "I won't make you keep your hands to yourself," she promised with a wink.

Shit, he couldn't take it any longer. Taking Shea by the hand, Craig got up from the couch and took her in the direction he thought her bedroom was in. "Come on let's get packing so we can go."

The light sound of her laughter followed by Shea pulling at her hand made him stop in his tracks. "What are you laughing at?" Had he said something funny? If he had he wanted to know what it was.

"Sweetheart, I can't pack now. I have to see if one of my neighbors can get my mail. I need to leave my contract information with Wanda, and besides, shouldn't you let Josh know about our trip?" she replied then placed a kiss by the corner of his mouth.

Why did she have to be so right? Craig wondered as her words set in his head. He did need to go over a few things with Josh before he escaped with Shea.

The trip would be good for the both of them. It was past time they let their guard down and explored this passion between them. Shea wasn't going to leave this trip until they had everything settled and out in the open. Craig was feeling more than a little guilty that Shea didn't know about the information Mr. Terry had given him. He would make a point of coming clean to her while they were on the trip.

When he looked at Shea now, the word 'wife' kept flashing before his eyes. In the past couple of weeks, Shea had opened up to him, but he still thought she might be holding something back. He wouldn't stay in limbo like this any longer. He wanted Shea in his life for as long as she would allow it.

Do you really want her, or are you deceiving yourself? his mind taunted. Craig shoved down the wayward thought. No, he honestly cared about Shea and wanted her in his life. She was the woman that crossed his T's and dotted his I's. He wasn't using her for an alternative purpose. In his heart and the deepest part of his soul, he knew Shea balanced him out. However, he only had to find a way to make his mind believe it as well.

"Sweetheart, what has put that look on your face?" Shea asked, drawing his attention back to her. She ran a finger over the wrinkle that usually appeared in his forehead when he worried too much.

He captured her hand, placing a kiss on the inside of her wrist. The sensual scent of raspberry stirred his cock making him aroused all over again. *Wonderful, another night filled with cold showers and no sleep.*

"Nothing, honey," he lied, hoping to keep her questions at bay.

"Don't lie to me. I can tell you're upset about something. Why won't you tell me about it? Aren't you supposed to confide in your girlfriend when you're having a problem?"

His heart pounded at hearing Shea address herself as his girlfriend; Craig loved how that one word relaxed the stress in his body. "Honey, I'm not lying to you. I was just deep in thought. I'm sorry I worried you. Do I need to stay here and make it up to you," he asked seductively.

A flicker of interest flashed in her sinful eyes, and then disappeared. "No, I need you to leave." Taking him by the hand, Shea hauled him off the couch and walked him in the direction of the door. "You're tempting me way too much late as it is."

Opening the front door, she laid her hand in the middle of his chest and gently shoved him out. "Good night, Craig. I'll see you on Friday."

"Why can't I see you until Friday?" Craig complained, bracing his hand on the doorframe, so Shea couldn't move him. "I don't want to wait a whole twenty-four hours before I see you again. Can't I take you out to lunch tomorrow or maybe a late dinner?" he suggested, grasping for straws.

"No, we both have to take care of things before our romantic weekend and besides the time apart will make our desire for each other hotter."

"I don't think I can get any hotter for you," Craig complained, fighting the urge to beg. "I know you want me to stay," he said, giving her a wounded look.

"Don't you give me that lost puppy look because it isn't going to work on me," Shea mused, moving moved his arm off the doorframe. She pushed him completely away from the door and closed it in his face.

Craig stared at the closed door, then laughed "Okay, I'll give you that round, but I'll get you back for that Shea," he promised through the closed door.

Chapter Eighteen

Go get him. Shea hurried away from the door so her body wouldn't act out what her mind hungered for. Why did she let Craig walk out that door? Was her head screwed on tight? He was the catch of the year, and she practically shoved him out the door. What she was doing was difficult, but she had to make him see that she wasn't like the others. He wasn't going to use those powerful good looks to sweep her off her feet. She wouldn't allow him to make her another one of his arm pieces.

She had her own dreams, and she needed a clear mind to work on the bed and breakfast. Pierre had done her part, and now it was her turn to get things figured out on her end.

Owning a B&B had been part of her five-year plan, and with the money Rebecca left her it could become a reality, but how would she break the news to Craig? He hadn't brought up the stocks in a while, but that didn't mean he had forgotten about them. Craig would always be a businessman first, unless he fell hard for a woman, and an enormous part of her wanted to be that woman.

Craig was under the illusion that she was going to sign over *Luscious Lips* stocks over to him in a couple of weeks, but after giving it careful consideration she was going to take the money and use it.

A twinge of guilt hit her for not coming clean about her plans to Craig when he was here, but the bed and breakfast was still so much up in the air. She didn't want to jinx anything by bragging about it too soon. Plus she couldn't get the words to come out of her mouth at all while he was sitting there next to her.

Shuffling around the house, Shea cleaned up the fruit tray she made for Pierre. Carrying it inside the kitchen, she tossed it into the trashcan and laughed at the thought of Pierre and her different weight loss plans. How could someone who was already a size eight want to lose any more weight? Nevertheless, being the good friend she was she helped Pierre out.

Pierre was the adventurous one in their relationship; however, she was beginning to think some of it was rubbing off on her. The old timid Shea that first met Craig wouldn't be planning a weekend getaway with him. Yet, with the new confidence she had gained over the past few weeks, she was ready for anything.

She finished with her housework and made her way towards her bedroom. After a quick shower, she pulled on her favorite lavender nightgown. Falling down on the mattress, she found her journal under the pillow and started working on her latest entry.

Dear Journal,

I had the biggest scare of my life today. I almost lost my bed and breakfast home. I hadn't wanted to spend any of the money Rebecca left to me, but after the news Pierre told me I'm going to cash in some of those stocks. I'll get eight hundred thousand dollars and still have money left over.

A thought crossed my mind and I hope it works. I was thinking about using the Luscious Lips *products at the B&B. Maybe have a section with gifts baskets that guests could buy at a cheaper price, and then if it works go from there.*

I have so many ideas for my dream job that I want to run past Craig, but I knew tonight wasn't the perfect time to do it. He wanted intimacy and I didn't give it to him. I'm surprised that he left as quietly as he did. I thought he might have tried to seduce me one last time before he left.

Having Craig's warm body pressing me into the sofa cushions almost did me in, but I gathered what strength I had and sent him on his way. It was hard, but I did it. I wonder why it's getting harder for me to tell him no?

Hmmm....I know what it is....I love him.

Shea's mouth pulled into a smile as she closed her journal and laid it on the dresser next to her bed. "I can't afford to stay up late tonight. I've a lot to get done tomorrow, plus I want to dream about Craig." Sliding between the sheets, she adjusted the covers over her body and closed her eyes for a night filled with dreams of Craig.

* * * *

"I can only imagine what you're going to do on this trip." Josh taunted, falling down into a chair inside Craig's bedroom. "You better be sure you carry enough protection with you unless you want a little Shea running around next year."

Craig tossed a couple of shirts inside his bag before he answered Josh. "Don't worry, I'm well-prepared for that. I'm not ready for kids, but I won't mind having some with Shea. She's gorgeous, but more than that I'm in love with her."

"Are you really?"

He turned around at the sound of his friend's voice and the disbelief that lingered there. "What makes you say that? Shea is very important to me. Why do you think I planned this trip?"

"To seduce her so you can get the stocks back in your name. Don't forget, you told me how you felt about her when Rebecca first introduced the two of you."

He hated when Josh constantly brought up things from the past. It made his blood boil, and sometimes he thought twice about making Josh his sounding board. But he needed to let steam off back then, and Josh listened to him. He wouldn't ever forget that.

Hell, Josh even gave him the kick in the ass he needed by asking Shea out on a date. After the initial shock of jealousy wore off, he figured out that Josh was never interested in Shea. But if Josh had been, he would make sure it wouldn't have lasted. Shea was his. A ring belonged around her finger, and he was going to be the only man to place it there.

"Can't you leave that conversation in the past?" he sighed. "There's no need for Shea to ever know about that bad idea I had. She's falling for me, and nothing will mess this up, do you understand?" Craig eyed Josh until he squirmed in his seat and let out a nervous cough. "Don't do anything to ruin it."

"I hope that is true, because if Shea finds out the truth your relationship with her would be over in an instant," Josh reminded him.

Craig reached across the bed and grabbed two pair of jeans, then tossed them into his bag. "Will you shut up about that? Shea will never find out about that," he insisted. "I was wrong to even think I could do that to her. I love her so much now, and nothing is going to ruin that. Do you understand me?"

Josh gave him a disbelieving look. "Do you really think this will stay a secret? God, you can't even be honest with yourself," he argued.

"What are you talking about?" Craig pitched the black bag containing his shaving kit on top of his jeans.

"You keep preaching over and over how much you're in love with Shea and how being with her has changed your life, but that's a lie and we both know it," Josh exclaimed.

Craig didn't like how Josh was talking to him. His soon-to-be former best friend didn't know anything about his relationship with Shea. Josh needed to keep his mouth closed when it came to Shea, because he wouldn't have a problem closing it for him.

"Stop talking in circles and get to the point. I know that you can," he complained, zipping up his bag. "I'm going to be late picking up Shea." It had taken a tremendous amount of willpower for him not to call or go by her house yesterday, so he was more than ready to kiss those full lips of hers.

"What did she say when you told about the clause in the will Mr. Terry told you about?" Josh tossed out.

Why was Josh picking at him like this? His buddy knew when crossed, his temper could be almost uncontrollable, and he seemed destined to feel the power of it today before he left.

"You know I haven't told her about that, so why are you even asking me?"

"Are you going to tell her or will you let it be a surprise to her? You know that she'll never look at you the same again." Josh pointed out, making him feel bad.

"Don't judge me when you can't tell the truth, either," he replied, sharply tossing his bag on the floor. "You need a woman so you'll keep your nose out of my business. Maybe if you had some woman problems of your own you wouldn't be so interested in my love life."

Josh shot him a cold look. "No thank you. I don't want a woman leading me around by the nose like Shea does you. Besides, I don't think there is a woman out there that could win me over."

Struggling not to laugh, Craig walked over and patted his envious friend on the shoulder. "Don't worry, your day will come, and when it does I'm going to laugh my head off."

A hand reached up and brushed his touch off. "I'm serious. I'm going to stay single for the rest of my life. There are too many sexy women out there for me to settle down with only one. Marriage isn't for me, so don't get any ideas about finding me a wife. The only wedding I want to attend is yours."

Craig stared down at Josh, who was trying his best to keep the vacant look on his face. "Are you telling me you didn't notice how cute Shea's friend Pierre was?"

Josh's expression changed the second Pierre's name left Craig's mouth. "No, I didn't notice her. Hell, why would I want to notice a woman with a guy's name?"

Josh was hiding something from him, but he didn't have time to get into it. After he got back home from his vacation Josh would tell him everything. Moving back from Josh, he hesitated and rethought his idea.

"Did something happen between you and Pierre after the two of you left Shea's the other night?" He didn't want Josh playing around with Pierre like he did with other women. Shea's friend wasn't a booty call waiting to happen. If Josh won over Pierre with his charm and then dumped her, it might end up ruining his relationship with Shea.

Crossing one leg over the other, Josh leaned back in the chair without answering his question. He hated when Josh got smug like this. "Don't sit there. You *damn well* better answer me. I don't want to spend my trip waiting while Shea answers phone calls from Pierre. I'm going to ask you one last time. Did you sleep with Pierre?"

"No, I didn't sleep with Pierre after we left Shea's," Josh said. "I'm not going to lie and say that I didn't try to get her to have drinks with me, but she turned me down cold."

Excellent!

"I'm sorry that happened to you. I know that you usually don't get shot down like that," Craig laughed, then quickly cleared his throat to cover it up.

"Hell, I don't care that it happened. It isn't like I can't find another woman to ask out on a date. I'm successful, semi-wealthy with a nice car, body, and a killer smile. I think I'll be a shoe in for a dance tonight at the club."

Hearing Josh talk about the dating scene made Craig remember parts of his past that he longed to forget. Shea showed him that he didn't have to be perfect all the time and there was nothing wrong with a few mistakes here and there along the way.

"I'll remind you of this conversation when you're waiting for your bride to walk down the aisle," Craig taunted.

"How about you leave me alone and focus the conversation back on you and Shea? I'm still blown away by how fast your relationship came together. One minute the two of you were yelling at each other and now you're going away on a trip."

How could he explain his relationship to Josh? "I've always been half in love with her, but I didn't want to admit it to myself. She's perfect for me."

"I hope you're right about all of this," Josh sighed.

"I know I'm right, now get up off your lazy ass and walk me to my car. I've got to pick up Shea in thirty minutes and I don't want to be late," Craig said, reaching for his suitcase.

* * * *

"Are you sure about this?" Pierre asked, staring down at the papers Shea just handed her. "Shouldn't you let Craig know about this first? He might not like finding out about this after the fact."

Shea waved her hand at Pierre. "Stop being such a worrier. Craig said he doesn't care about the money anymore, so I'm going to use it for the bed and breakfast. I want to make an official bid on that house. Didn't you tell me I had time before the other buyers came back into town?"

"Yeah, I did say that, but this is an awfully high offer. Shouldn't you start low and work your way up to this?" Pierre complained. "I don't want to force you into doing something you might regret later."

"Pierre, you're a wonderful friend and I'm very happy you're concerned about me, but I'm not nervous about starting my own business or Craig's reaction. He said that he was in love with me, and this will prove if he was lying to me." Shea prayed with every fiber in her body that Craig wasn't trying to pull the wool over her eyes, but if he was, that was his problem and not hers.

"I still can't believe Craig told you that," Pierre said, walking to her briefcase on the sofa and shoving her paperwork inside. "Did you tell him that you were in love with him, too?"

"No."

"Why not?" Pierre tossed Shea a look. "You are in love with him, aren't you?"

"Of course I am, but I want to make sure everything is on point between us before I say those three little words. I've never told a man that before and hopefully Craig will be the only man I tell."

"After the way he acted at your apartment the other night, I'm sure he'll wait until you're ready to tell him. He's head over heels in love with you. I still can't believe you didn't tell him I was a woman." Pierre giggled.

Shea smiled at the memory. It felt good to see Craig all fired up about her being with another guy. "He never gave me the chance to tell him. He just heard your name and assumed I was cheating on him. How can I cheat on him when we haven't even made love yet?"

"I'm pretty sure that problem will be solved tonight once Craig gets you all alone," Pierre winked.

"Stop it. You are just too crazy," Shea laughed.

"Well, you're going to think I'm out of my mind when I show you the present I have for you."

"What are you talking about?" She watched Pierre retrieved a small bag out of her oversized purple purse. "What is that?"

"I wanted your trip with Craig to be something to have wonderful memories of so, I brought you a gift," Pierre confessed shoving the bag in her direction. "Open it."

"Pierre, what have you done?" Shea asked, taking the bag.

"Something that you wouldn't have done for yourself," she teased, looking at her. "Craig is going to love it if you have enough confidence to wear it for him."

"God, I don't want to know." Opening the bag, Shea stuck her hand inside and tugged a small scrap of red and orange fabric. Her eyes grew wide at the lack of material in her hand, and she watched her friend standing mere inches in front of her.

"You can't be serious," she gasped, waving the nightie around.

"Hey, you want to keep him coming back for more, don't you? A man like Craig looks like he has a healthy appetite and you need to stop acting like the shy virgin. We both know that you've had sex before."

"Sure I have, yet this is a bit much even for me. I love wearing sexy underclothes, but I like everything to be supported. This isn't going to hold the girls up at all. I'll be spilling out all over the place, and I'm not that voluptuous."

Grinning, Pierre clapped her hands together. "That's the reason I got it. Men are so visual and Craig won't be able to get past what's popping out not to notice you might not be a double D."

"I'll give it a try," Shea said, weakening to the idea of Craig lusting after her even more. It did make her feel good to know she had that kind of power over him. "But don't buy me anymore of these crazy things," she exclaimed, shoving the garment back into the bag. "I can't let him get the wrong idea."

"What kind of wrong idea can Craig get from my present?" Pierre asked, eyeing her.

"That I wear clothes to bed," she answered with a straight face, then broke out in laughter when Pierre eyebrows rose up to her hairline.

"Oh, you're such a bad girl. Maybe I need to take some pointers from you so I can get a man. I'm three years older than you and without the possibility of a real relationship in sight."

"Maybe I'll ask Craig to fix you up with one of his friends from work. Come to think of it, I don't think Josh is dating anyone and he's very attractive."

Pierre wrinkled her nose like a bad taste suddenly appeared in her mouth. "Thanks, but no thanks. I don't want Josh. He's too smug for me. He thinks a woman was made to fall at his feet. Do you know he had the nerve to ask me out for drinks after we left your house?"

"I don't have to ask what your answer was, do I?" Shea strolled across the room and shoved her present inside the side opening of her carry-on bag. It had been a present from Rebecca before she died. She was so glad that she accepted the expensive bag now.

"Of course, I told him no and left him standing there in the middle of the sidewalk," Pierre admitted, "but I have to agree with you, he's very handsome."

"Handsome enough for you to overlook that one bad quality of his?" Shea inquired. "If I hadn't looked past Craig's cockiness, I might not be going away with him."

"Don't have an answer for you," Pierre answered honestly. "Ask me after your getaway and I might do that blind date thing for you."

"Good, I'll let Craig know and make sure he doesn't try to force Josh under your radar. By the way, have I thanked you for agreeing to stay here while I was gone?"

"No, you didn't, but that doesn't matter. I know you would do the same thing for me," Pierre replied. "I better go and lock up my house. If you aren't here when I get back have a fantastic time with your man.

Make sure that when the trip is over Craig can't live without you."

Shea wrapped her arm around Pierre's shoulder and escorted her to the door. "I think he already feels that away. However, it wouldn't hurt to deepen it." Opening the door, she gave her friend another hug before Pierre stepped off the porch and headed for her car. She waved goodbye to Pierre as her friend got into her car, then drove off.

Closing the door, she moved back into the room and sat on the empty seat beside her purse. Shea crossed her fingers and propped her chin down on them. She looked around the room and let her mind meander about how good her life was now. A few short months ago she wished Craig would get over his hate of her and notice her as a desirable woman. It happened, and she couldn't be happier about it.

"My life is so good now. I can't see how it could get any better. I'm going to own my own business. I have a considerate, understanding, and damn sexy boyfriend," Shea said out loud. "The only thing that is missing is a ring on my finger, and I don't mind waiting for that.

Chapter Nineteen

Hearing a familiar rapid knock on the front door, Shea jumped up from the couch and raced over to it. She flung it open and threw herself into Craig's arms. His mouth crashed down on her, almost taking her breath. His tongue explored the roof and corners of her mouth, making her banked need for him explode and grow hotter. She felt the heaviness of yearning settle over her body and moisture pooled between her thighs.

Groaning, she locked her legs around Craig's waist and slid her hands through his hair, holding him to her and brushing her lips over his some more. A low growl broke from his mouth as he cupped her ass in his hand. His teeth nipped at her bottom lip.

The kiss was urgent and hungry. It showed how much the two of them wanted each other and how the waiting period was over. There was no doubt in her mind the two of them would be one, but would they be able to last until they got to their destination?

Craig moved his mouth over hers, devouring its softness. Raising his mouth from hers, he gazed into her eyes with such a burning need that she bit her lip to keep from moaning.

"You told me having a day apart would make things hotter and you were correct. I can't believe how much I've missed you," he confessed, lifting her body off his. "If I don't get my senses under control I might forget that we are outside on your porch."

"Omigod." She quickly looked around Craig and noticed three of her nosiest neighbors standing in their yards, staring at her. "I can't believe I did that," she gasped, yanking Craig into the house and then implied. "I won't be able to show my face out there again. They already hate the fact I got this house. Now I've given them something juicy to talk about."

"I love when things are juicy, wet, and slippery," Craig whispered, easing his hand inside her jeans. "I think the wetter the better," he continued as his fingers snuck into her underwear and teased her wet curls.

"Oh..." She moaned, reaching for Craig's hand. "We can't do this." Hot desire shot through her as two long fingers thrust into her, filling her completely.

Keeping his hand inside her pants, Craig backed her up until she was pressed against the door. "I think we have all the time in the world, baby," he whispered, running his tongue alongside her neck. "I can't let you ride in the car for hours with this need clawing at you. You need a release, and I'm just the man to give it to you."

"No, I can't let you do this," she panted as Craig's free hand started to unsnapped the buttons on her shirt. "It isn't fair to you."

"Don't worry about me. Watching you find your pleasure will only enhance mine," he swore as his thumb brushed over her wetness, setting off another wave of spiraling need.

Shea stared into Craig's face and saw how his eyes had grown darker and more intense since he had taken control of the situation. It was like being the dominant one gave him an extra thrill.

As much as his words touched a part of her that hadn't been stroked in a while, she still wanted them to combust together when it was time. "No, Craig. I'm serious about this," she replied, removing his hand from her jeans. "I want us to be together when it happens. My pleasure will last longer if you're with me." Shea slipped around Craig's large body and fixed her clothes. She knew the second he had come to stand behind her because his nearness was overwhelming. She couldn't keep the tingle of excitement from wrapping around her when Craig's arms circled her waist.

"I love you more and more each day," he sighed. "I don't know how I made it this long without you."

It made her feel so good to hear that, she was glad to be with him, too. "Darling, I couldn't have said it any better," Shea whispered, running her fingers over the hairs on his arms.

"Can't you tell me that you love me?" he breathed by her neck. "I know that you do."

"You're right, I do, but I can't say it just yet. I will," she promised.

Craig tried to hide his disappointment from her, but she was aware of it from the way his body tensed. "I'm not a patient man, but I can wait a little longer to hear the words," he said and then stepped away from her. "Is that all you're carrying?" He pointed at her two bags by the door. "I thought most females needed at least five more than that."

"I'm not like any of the women you have dated," she teased, tapping Craig on the arm.

"You're right. None of them held my heart in the palm of their hands like you do," he answered as he went over to her bags and picked them up. "How about we go ahead and leave?"

Making one final check of her house, she gathered the rest of her belongings and made her way over to Craig. He was still hurt by her lack of words, and she hated that. She swore to herself to make it up to him tonight. "Let's hit the road. I can't wait until I see what you have planned for us." Shea stopped in front of Craig and gave him a quick kiss on the mouth.

"I love kissing you. You taste so good," she moaned. "I could kiss you for hours."

"Baby, I feel the same way about you," Craig said "The sweet taste of your lips is addictive. Would you rather stay here? We have enough time to burn off this extra energy."

No...if they made love here there was no way in hell they would ever leave the house. "Sorry, I shouldn't have started this," she apologized. "I want to leave. I can't wait to see what you've planned for us."

Craig groaned under his breath "I hate that you're the level headed one. You've to keep me in line or I might steal a kiss or two while we're on the road."

"I might keep you in line or I might not," she teased. "It all depends what mood I'm in. I might the one who steals a kiss or two myself."

"Woman...stop teasing me."

She pushed Craig outside and she followed him, making sure the door was locked. Standing on the steps, Shea watched Craig load her bags into the trunk with his. "Don't you worry, Craig, when this trip is over you will know how much you mean to me," she promised, taking a deep breath.

* * * *

Resting her head against the seat, Shea listened to the CD playing in the car stereo. The soft, soothing sounds of Gerald Levert calmed her body and relaxed her nerves. As they drove down the highway she took in the beauty of fall in Maine. It was the most perfect time of the year. She loved all the brilliant colors of the leaves changing along with the clean, fresh crisp air that made her body feel more invigorated.

A rainbow of colors ranging from orange, gold, yellow, and red covered the trees that spread across the highway. She wasn't much of a hiker, but she didn't doubt the beauty of the woods would take her breath away. Fall always made her want to pick apples for fresh pies or hold a cup of hot cider in front of the fireplace.

"What has that pretty little head of yours thinking so hard?" Craig asked, placing his hand on her leg.

Laying her hand on top of his, she linked their fingers together. "Apples pies and hot apple cider," she confessed.

"Aunt Rebecca made the best homemade apple pies. When I was a little kid she always made sure I got the last slice with two scoops of vanilla ice cream."

"My mother did the same thing for me, and it used to make my little brother so mad, so I shared it with him."

"Weren't you a good big sister," Craig replied, squeezing her hand. "I bet you were beautiful then as you are now."

Shea recalled how she looked when she was younger and her mouth turned up at the memory. "No, I had braces and wore these huge glasses because I had eye problems. I finally had laser surgery my freshman year of college and got that fixed. It was the best thing I ever did."

"I bet I would have fallen in you love with you even then. I'm not in love with the outside shell, but the beauty the lies inside of you," he responded, stealing a quick glance at her.

"You sure know how to make a woman feel special and loved," Shea said, resting her head on Craig's wide shoulder.

"I want to make you feel more than that, but now isn't the time to get into it," Craig said, drawing her attention to his profile. "We can discuss it later."

Is he going to ask me to marry him? Easing her head off him, Shea studied Craig from underneath her lashes. Would she say yes if he were to pop the question? Had they gotten to know each other well enough to become husband and wife? It only took her a half a second to come up with an answer.

Yes, yes and yes. She would accept Craig's marriage proposal in a hot mega second. "Are you sure you don't want to go into it now? We aren't doing anything important and I'm ready to listen."

Craig looked into the rearview mirror, and turned on his signal. Pulling over to the side of the hideaway, he shut off the engine and faced her. "Do you really want to hear what I've to tell you?"

"Yes."

* * * *

How could he tell this amazing woman the truth? He only started dating her at first for his aunt's stocks? No, he couldn't do it. Craig didn't want to spend this trip trying to find a way to win her back. Without a doubt if he told her the truth now, Shea would be out of his life so quickly that he would forget his own name. He vowed to fulfill each and every one of her fantasies for the entire weekend, and telling her the truth now would prevent that for happening.

On this trip Shea should enjoy herself fully and thoroughly, plus secretly he hoped to learn more about her dreams, likes, dislikes and wishes. Maybe he could help her accomplish some of them in the process.

Craig traced the corners of Shea's mouth with his finger, and his stomach jumped when her tongue licked the tip. He was falling hard for her and loving every minute. "I want to spend the nights making love until neither of us can remember the day of the week. Maybe if I get lucky enough you might even let us take a bath together.

"I want to do all the things a man does with the most important woman in his life," he continued, "if that doesn't turn you on, then I'm willingly to change it to a campfire under the moonlight sky with a millions of star shining above us. There isn't anything more important to me than spending every waking hour this weekend wrapped in your arms.

"I know you've told me not two hours ago that you aren't ready to tell me that you love me, but I'll keep screaming my love for you at the top of my lungs. Shea Antonia Anderson, I love you.

"Baby, don't cry," Craig said, brushing the tears away that trailed down Shea's silky cheek. "I didn't say that to make you cry."

"What else did you expect me to do after hearing those wonderful words?" she asked, touching his hands. "After that how can I not tell you that I'm in love with you, too?"

He didn't want to pressure Shea into admitting her feelings for him. They had to come from her freely or they wouldn't mean a thing. "Did I make you say that to me? I could have waited until you were ready to tell me."

"Craig, I love you. You can ask me that question a hundred times and the answer will always be the same. I'm in love with you, and I wasn't complete until you came into my life. I'm so very happy that I met Rebecca, because if I hadn't I wouldn't know the pleasure of loving you."

Satisfaction turned up the corners of his mouth as contentment soared through his veins. Shea was *in love* with him and he wasn't about to lose her anytime soon. "How about we get back on the road and headed to our destination before nightfall hits?"

"Sounds like a plan to me," Shea sighed, snuggling up closer to him. "Let's hit that road and leave everything else in our dust."

Starting the car, Craig checked to make sure everything was clear before pulling out back onto the road. "Romantic paradise, here we come," he shouted then placed a kiss on the side of Shea's head.

* * * *

For the next hour Craig listened as Shea filled the time with entertaining stories from her childhood. He loved hearing the excitement in her voice at the memories. He especially loved the stories of when she was a little girl and loved playing hide and seek in the house with her mother. Or the time she stayed outside a little longer than she should and got a spanking from her mother.

Craig loved how Shea was sharing this part of her life with him. It gave him more insight on how her mind worked. How could he ever think she was anything worse but the giving person that she was?

He had wished for months to be alone with her, and now he finally had his chance. He only hoped the place he picked was romantic enough. Several places had run through his mind, like an isolated Greek Island, the Poconos, Italy, or Cancun, but they didn't have enough time to do any of those places justice, so he settled for a quiet little getaway.

An idealistic vacation to him consisted of being together with that unique person. Where you could explore all your surroundings, get dressed up and go out to eat at a fancy restaurant. Another part of his plan was to take a lot of pictures so he'd have something to remember the trip by. He might even help Shea make a scrapbook and keep it so they could show their children how they fell more in love with each other.

Craig didn't know how he became such a hopeless romantic in such a short period of time, but he loved it and wouldn't change a thing. Shea better be prepared because he wasn't going to let her leave this weekend until she agreed to become his wife.

Chapter Twenty

"Are you sure this place is ours for the next three days?" Shea asked, racing towards the front of the cottage. "I can't believe how stunning it is, with the lake in front of us."

It better be theirs with the extra money he had to throw in at the very last minute to keep two other couples from sharing the place with them. "Baby, it's ours for the next three days. If you want to walk around naked feel free to do so," he yelled at her retreating form.

Shea stopped on the gravel trail and tossed him a look over her shoulder. "You should be so lucky, and after a comment like that you might be sleeping on the couch," she teased back.

Running after the cute little temptress in front of him, Craig picked Shea up and laid her down on the thick grass. "Don't tease me like that. I'm a hungry man and all this waiting is killing me. I'm not sure I can wait much longer."

"Oh, is my Craig all hot and bothered? Should I kiss it and make it all better?"

"Kiss it, touch it, lick it, squeeze it, anything you want to do that will make it better," he growled, pulling Shea's hands above her head. "I can't deny you anything, woman. I'll strip naked right this

142

second and let you have your way with me. I'll even be your slave for life if that is what you want."

Biting her bottom lip, Shea looked like she was pondering his idea. "I never had a man at my beck and call before. It might be fun to have one now. Do you do windows and floors?"

He shook his head and leaned into Shea's soft curves more. "No, I'm more of a one on one kind of servant."

Getting into their little game, Shea wiggled her body under his and his cock shot to attention. He loved how she never missed a beat when it came to role playing with him.

"Do you mind if I ask what is your field of expertise? I can't have anyone inside of my...house," she whispered, "without having a little background check first. Do you know how to please your customer and have them begging you to come back for a second round?"

"I'm at the top of my field so I don't do second rounds. I automatically go into the third and final round. Are you up to that or should I move slower with you? I don't mind a training period." He would go at any paced she needed.

"I don't need a training period. I can handle anything you toss my way, Craig. I'm more than prepared for an all-nighter if need be."

Shit!

Shea was hot and more experienced than he thought. It was going to be a better night than he first believed. "We'll see how round one goes and move on from there," Craig suggested, getting up off the ground and tugging Shea up behind him. "I think I should show you the rest of the place, and then we can decide what to do next."

"Well, don't keep me waiting," Shea sighed and raced past him to the front of the cottage.

Catching up with her, Craig wrapped his arm around Shea's waist, walking with her the rest of the way. He pointed out the two white wood lounge chairs positioned in front of the covered patio. "I love these. We can sit out here and watch people out on the water. If you get the urge we can even go out there on some jet skis."

"I've never been on a jet ski before," Shea confessed. "Is it dangerous?"

"No, it's a lot of fun and I'll make sure everything is perfect before I let you get on one. I have to protect the woman I love, don't I?"

"I guess you do," she agreed with a huge smile.

"Okay, enough of that smile of yours or I'm not going to be able to wait for us to make love," he exclaimed, shaking off the effect Shea constantly had on his body. Craig made his mind move back to the tour he wanted to give her. "Around on the other side is a nice sized flower bed. I think you might see some flowers there you might like to look at."

"Is the inside as stunning as the outside?" Shea asked, strolling across the rich green grass. "I love how it looks out here."

Craig treasured that Shea was jubilant. All he sought after from this trip to was her to place a smile on her face. It was all part of his master plan of seduction. "I know that I liked it when I saw the pictures on the Internet."

Making their way across the grass, Craig opened the door to the outside patio and waited for Shea to slip past him. Without giving it a second thought, he ran his hand over her tight, round ass. "You are so damn sexy. I'm going to have the hardest time keeping my hands off you this weekend."

"The same goes for me," Shea replied, her gaze raking up and down his body. "I didn't know a pair of jeans and a black shirt could look so good on a man."

"I don't want to brag, but I look even better without them," he answered, stepping into the patio with her. "Are you ready to see?"

Shea closed the slight space between them and wrapped her arms around his neck. "How about you finish giving me a tour of our getaway cottage and fix me something good to eat? Because I want to be well nourished for the night you have planned for us."

Craig ran his hands up and down Shea's back for a few minutes enjoying, the scent of the fresh air and the remarkable woman in his arms. Moving his fingers down a little further, Craig kneaded the perfect form of her ass one more time. "Are you telling me that you want us to stay here and not go into town for dinner?"

He was on cloud nine if Shea would rather spend their first night here alone away from the prying eyes of other people. However, if she wanted to go out for a nice little candlelight dinner in a restaurant, then he would do that, too. These next couple days were for Shea, and anything she had in her pretty little head to do.

"Do we have enough food here? I really don't want to share you with the rest of the world this weekend. I want this to be our time."

Craig couldn't agree more. He could stay locked away out here with her, too, making love all different hours of the day or just lying around and talking to each other. "I told the owners to stock the cabinets so we should have enough food for the next three days and then some," he said, caressing Shea's body. "So, how about I finish this tour later? I can throw us a quick meal together and then the rest of the night is ours."

"You won't hear any complaints from me," Shea sighed, kissing his on the side of the mouth before she took a step back.

"Okay, you go into the kitchen and find us something to eat. I'll get the bags out and take them to our room." Craig couldn't get over that tonight he would be spending the night with the woman of his dreams. He couldn't ask for a more perfect day if he had three wishes.

"I would love to do that, but we have one little problem," Shea frowned.

"What kind of problem do we have?"

"I don't have a clue where the kitchen is in this place," she laughed, placing her hand in the middle of his chest. "How about you give me some directions? Once I get there I can find anything I need. I'm pretty good in the kitchen," Shea bragged.

Craig groaned at his own stupidity. "Baby, go straight through the door behind you and it's the first door on your left."

146

"See you in a few minutes," Shea replied, taking her hand off of him and disappearing through the door.

On the way back to the car, Craig thought about how to ask Shea to marry him and the one scenario she would cherish the most years from now. Taking their luggage out of the trunk, he brought them back in the house through the family room. Craig paused in the spacious room, smiling at the sound of Shea signing as she moved around in the kitchen.

Chuckling softly, he continued on and made his way up the spiral staircase. Placing the bags on the bed, he went into the bathroom and washed his hands, then hurried back down stairs to Shea.

She shouldn't spend the first night of their vacation inside the kitchen working. If he had known she wouldn't have wanted to go out, he would have hired a cook to prepare a meal for them.

Relaxing in the doorway, Craig crossed his arms over his chest, and ran his gaze over the soft contours of Shea's body. He watched as she dropped a piece of chicken into a hot skillet. The smell brought back memories of summers spent with his aunt. "I love fried chicken, but I seldom fixed it for myself."

"Why not?" Shea inquired, spinning around to face him.

Craig grinned at the white line of flour going across her left cheek. Coming into the room, he brushed it off with his fingertips, then kissed her silky smooth skin. "I'm not good at frying it, and I don't have the patience to wait until it's done. If I have a taste for it I usually go get it at a drive-through."

"That is the saddest thing I've ever heard," Shea laughed. She eased around him and washed her hands off in the sink. "I'm going to give you a cooking lesson, so you won't starve without around you."

"Food isn't what I'm hungry for at the moment," he growled, moving to stand behind her at the sink. "I need something else more fulfilling to end this hunger that is buried deep inside of me."

"Do you want me to make you some homemade biscuits to go along with the food?" Shea teased, turning around so they were facing each other. "You need to let me know so I can get started."

"Woman, you know that wasn't the type of nourishment I was referring to," he said, touching Shea's erect nipples through her thin sweater. "Your body knows what I want."

Purring, Shea played with the buttons on his shirt, giving him a smothering look. "Let me get something to eat first and I'll show you how much my body wants yours," she promised.

He was shocked and pleased by the way Shea was reacting to him. "I didn't know you had this side in you. You always came across as a little timid or shy."

"I'm not either of those things, but I wasn't about to throw myself at you, either. Not when you complained about me every chance you got. I knew how to take a hint and leave you alone."

"Can I apologize now for the jerk I was back then to you? I never meant to come across like that, but I was so attracted to you that I couldn't see straight.

Plus you acted like you hated the sight of me," he said matter-of-factly.

Shea shrugged and then slipped away from him, going back over to the hot skillet. She flipped over the chicken, showing off a golden brown crisp. His mouth watered at the thought of the first bite of the juicy and crisp meat, but he had something to take care of first.

"How about I find a way to make my past behavior up to you?" he suggested. "Do you want me to write *I'm Sorry* a hundred times or how about a dozen roses for a month? Anything you want, just name it and it will be yours, even if I've to move Heaven and Earth to get it."

"I don't want you to do anything but for you to be yourself and treat me with respect and love," she replied, adding more chicken to the hot oil.

"That isn't a hard request at all, because I already love the hell out of you, but my love for you can always grow and get deeper," Craig answered with a quiet emphasis.

"Mr. Evans, you have a way with words. I think you went into the wrong profession. How about you set the table and find us something to drink," she suggested. "I think I saw plates over there in the cabinet next to the sink."

"I'm only like this with you, babe," he corrected, loving the homey feel of working with Shea in the kitchen. Moving to stand behind his woman, he planted a quick kiss on the back of her neck and then stepped away so he could set the table.

Minutes passed while Craig and Shea took care of dinner. After everything was done they sat down at the table and enjoyed a fun, carefree meal. All the problems from the week faded away as they stared into each others' eyes.

"How about we toss these dishes into the dishwasher and I'll take you into the living room?" Standing up, he cleared off the table and loaded the dishwasher, not wanting to miss another second that could be spent in Shea's arms.

"Can't wait to get me on the couch?"

"No, I can't wait to get you into my arms for our first dance. I saw a CD player and some CDs in there when I was on my way upstairs. Hopefully these people have some taste and I can slow dance with you." Craig grinned, taking Shea by the hand. He tugged her up from the chair. "I love anytime I get to touch you." A soft look came into Shea's eyes and Craig made a mental note to compliment her more.

"You better stop or I'll get a big head and start to believe there might be a long-term future for the two of us," she said, letting go of his hand. Shea tried to move past him into the other room but he stopped her.

"Why don't you think there could be something long-term between us?" He frowned. "Do you think I planned this weekend for a quick roll in the hay?" Craig hated the fact Shea wasn't sure of his commitment to her. "I want us to be together for as long as possible."

Soft fingers trailed down the side of his left cheek. "Let take things slow and see where it goes from there. I don't want us rushing into something and mess up what we already have. Now, how about that dance you promised me?" she asked, withdrawing her hand.

Yeah, you're going to be the one messing things up if you don't stop keeping things for her. Do you really think she's going to accept your proposal after she finds out the truth?

Craig shoved his subconscious out of his mind and linked his fingers with Shea's softer ones. "I think I already hear the music playing," he said, escorting her from the room.

Chapter Twenty-One

"What are you doing here? How did you know where I live in the first place?" Pierre frowned at Josh standing on the other side of her door as the fall wind blew at the ends of his hair. "Didn't I tell you I wasn't interested?"

One large, masculine shoulder rose up in a careless shrug, "What can I say? I liked the fact that you are playing hard to get," he said with an easy smile. "I've always found that quality attractive in a woman. Besides that, Craig thought we might hit it off if I got to know you better."

Pierre didn't want to admit that Shea practically told her the same thing before she left on her trip. "Craig doesn't know me that well to assume I would want to date someone like you."

Gray eyes flickered then drilled into hers, making her body take notice of the hunk in front of her. "What do you mean by someone like me?" Josh questioned in a heated voice.

"Do I really have to spell it out for you?"

"Are you talking about me being a white man? You didn't come across as a racist person to me."

Pierre didn't know whether to slam the door in Josh's face or laugh her head off at his assumption of her. "No, I could care less that you were white. My last two relationships were with white men. I'm talking about the fact that you're one of those men that still believe you're God's gift to women. I hate overly confident men."

"So, your last boyfriend allowed you lead him around by the nose, did he? Did he not know how to take charge of the situation? Or are you one of those women who get off wearing the pants in the relationship?"

"I get off on a lot of things, but you aren't one of them, Josh," she teased, enjoying the interested look that passed across his face.

"Are you challenging me to prove you wrong about that?" he asked. "I don't mind one bit taking you up on it. You're definitely the type of woman I'd love waking up to in the morning."

Pierre felt a shiver go through her body and she knew it wasn't from the cold air blowing around them. "I'm surprised you let any of your conquests spend the night after you're finished with them."

Josh stepped closer to her until his big body blocked out everything else. "I only let the special ones, and I can tell that you're going to be one of them."

"Don't assume. You know what they say about people who assume things that they shouldn't," she retorted trying to stay calm.

"No, I don't know what they say. Why don't you tell me?" he whispered, stroking the side of her face with the back of his hand like he had all the right to be touching her.

She shook off his light caress and glared at him above her reading glasses. "When you assume you make an ass of you and me. Are you going to tell me you never heard of that?"

"I can promise you that I'm not making an ass of myself. I'm very confident in my belief that you want me," Josh challenged without batting an eye. "Do you want me to prove it?"

No...no...don't let him prove it. "Sure, I have some time to kill," Pierre sassed back.

Josh's mouth was on hers the second the last word left hers, and Pierre almost fainted from the intense heat. All the built up sexual tension she hadn't been able to find with other men came crashing around her like an avalanche. One stroke, two strokes, three strokes, and she lost count of how many times Josh's tongue licked at hers.

She tried her best to shove Josh away from her but she couldn't do it. Instead her arms wrapped around his shoulders and pulled his hard body until her breasts pressed into his wide chest.

"Hell, get a room or at least go in the house, other people don't need to see that," a male voice yelled, breaking into their passionate moment.

The sound of the angry masculine voice was like a bucket of cold water poured over her head. Jerking back, Pierre pressed her trembling fingers to her swollen mouth. "This isn't going to happen again. I want you to stay away from me." She stepped back inside her house. "You aren't to breathe a word about this to Craig or anyone else."

"I'm not the type to kiss and tell, but this isn't over between us, Pierre, not by a long shot. I'll give you time to get yourself together, but I will be back,"

Josh promised, staring at her. "I liked what I sampled and I think…no, I know that I want another taste."

"Why?" she whispered.

"It was delicious and unique," Josh said matter of factly.

Pierre locked down her initial response, took a deep breath, and started over. "I wasn't talking about that. I don't understand why you want to come back after I shot you down three times already."

"You're like this huge thick maze of shrubs, and I can't wait until I get to the rose garden in the middle."

"I don't know what kind of game you're working on me, but I won't be a part of it. I'll ask nicely this time. Please leave me alone and romance another woman who's more willing than I am." She took one last lingering look at Josh and closed the door quietly, but not before she heard his final comment.

"You're willing you just don't know it yet."

Chapter Twenty-Two

Long fingers with dark hair dusting the knuckles slowly eased the buttons from her shirt and pushed it off her shoulders. It fell to the floor behind them as Lionel Richie's smooth voice filled the room. Spinning her around, Craig pressed his warm lips to the side of Shea's neck and stole a quick nibble.

"You smell so damn good. Did you smell this good on the car ride here?" he asked, moving his hands down her back, cupping her ass in his large palms. "Baby, I want you so bad I can't think straight."

"Not more than I want you," Shea replied while her fingers worked on the black buttons down his shirt. "I've been having these dreams about us."

"Dreams, or were they fantasies?" Craig questioned. "Were you naked in bed when these thoughts came into your mind? Was I there bringing your body to the brink, or was I just teasing you and making you beg for more?"

"God, that feels so good," he said as Shea ran her hands over his chest, pausing to play with his already rock hard nipples. "You shouldn't tease me like this, because payback will be a bitch."

"Who said I was playing with you?" Standing on her tiptoes, Shea drew his bottom lip into her mouth with her two front teeth, then sucked until he almost burst through his pants.

Where in the hell did she learn to kiss like this? Craig wondered as Shea's web of seduction wrapped him into a secluded paradise only meant for them. Night after night of cold showers never prepared him for the mind blowing reality of being like this with Shea.

Sliding his hand into her thick hair, he ended the wet kiss or things would have been over before they even started. "Baby, we have to stop. I don't want us to make love down here on a hard floor. There are so many better places."

"You are so right," she agreed, pushing his shirt off him. "We can make love on the table, the couch, in the chair by the window, or anywhere else that you might want to."

In the chair?

Shit, he'd make sure they did that one before they left on Sunday night. Shea was a lot more adventurous than he thought, and it was one hell of a turn-on for him. He fought down the bad boy side of his personality and said, "No, we have a nice comfortable bed upstairs."

"A bed sounds perfect," she retorted, then unsnapped the first hook on her bra, showing off a little more cleavage.

Craig moaned as his body grew even harder and stood up at attention at the scrumptious treats. He picked up Shea and tossed her over his shoulder. "You know better than to tempt me with those breasts of yours and not expect me to go crazy. Wait until I get you upstairs," he growled, slapping Shea on her tight ass as he practically raced towards the spiral staircase.

* * * *

Upstairs in the bedroom, Craig slid Shea down his body until her feet touched the floor. Placing a finger under her perky chin, he tilted her head back and stared into her liquid brown eyes. "I care about you more than I have any other woman. You're my soul mate, and everything I thought I would never find. Tonight will mean more to me than you will ever know."

"I feel the same way, too, baby," she mused, giving him a soft kiss.

Gathering her into his arms, he held Shea snugly to his body, against the rapid pounding of his heart. A brief shiver rippled through his body as her fingers played with the back of his neck, making his body more aware of hers.

Blood coursed through his veins down to his throbbing erection, and he smiled at the sharp intake of Shea's breath at the intimate contact. They had always shared an intense physical awareness of each other, but now he knew now how desperately he wanted to be deep inside of her tight body.

Craig was conscious of where his warm flesh brushed her smooth breasts, and the feel sent hot shivers of excitement all over his aroused body. Stepping back from his warm bundle of joy, he eased her bra and the rest of the clothes from her body, dropping them piece by piece on the floor until she stood naked in front of him.

He let his gaze ease over the contours of Shea's body, taking in the beauty mole to the right of her hipbone down to her hot pink toenails. He didn't want to leave an inch of her body untouched from his hot gaze. Reaching out, he held one perfect breast in the palm of his hand, testing its weight.

Shea hissed in an unsteady breath and squirmed under his seeking touch. She couldn't believe how fantastic it felt to have a man's hands on her body again. "Don't tease me like that, touch me," she begged.

"I plan to do more than that," he spoke softly, trying to make this moment last as long as he could. Back and forth he stroked his thumb over Shea's nipple, watching how the bud grew harder.

Whimpering she pressed her breast into his hand, "I'm aching so badly. Can't you do something about it?"

Gently he brushed a strand of hair away from Shea's mouth. It felt so perfect to be here with Shea like this. "I love being here like this with you. I feel so connected to you. I want this to last as long as it possibly can."

"Please touch me." The request was so soft and low that he almost missed it, but he had to make sure he heard correctly. Was Shea's body really weakening from his tender touches?

"Baby, what did you say?"

"Touch me," came the whispered request.

"Your wish is my command."

Craig was surprised and pleased that Shea asked him to touch her, because she had never done that before. Her body was so perfect that he was having a hard time deciding which part to enjoy first. Placing his hand palm down, he ran his fingers down the long column of her neck. He slowly stroked the racing pulse in her neck until a soft moan poured from her lips.

"I love you so much. I don't know what I've been doing with my life until you came into it," Craig whispered, moving to lick the outline of her ear.

"God, show me how much you love me," she begged, pulling at him. "Please, I can't take this ache. It's deep inside of me and you're the only person that can make it go away."

He wanted more than anything to give her the release she craved, but it wasn't time for that yet. Too many places on her body called for his attention and he planned to give each and every one of them pleasure tonight.

"Darling, you don't have to beg me for anything," he whispered, his breath hot against her ear. "I'm here for you and anything you want." Gathering her back in his arms, Craig laid Shea gently down on the bed and covered her body with his.

Shea tilted her head back and stared into his eyes. Without looking away, she ran her hand down the middle of his chest, stopping a breath away from his erection. "I want you to make me forget about anything that doesn't involve this moment. Make me the center of your world and I'll make you the center of mine later."

Not needing a second invitation, Craig leaned his body over Shea's, sliding one of his thighs between her soft legs. He got comfortable as he could with his raging erection. He made light circles around her left nipple, but made sure he didn't touch it. It puckered, demanding that he show it more attention. Bringing his fingers to his mouth, he licked the tips and brought them back down to the taut, brown nipple.

"Oh, don't do this," Shea panted, squirming as his fingers continued to tease and taunt her raised nipples.

"Do what?" he asked, replacing his fingers with his mouth.

Liquid brown eyes snapped shut as Shea twisted her head side to side on the pillow and her incredible legs spread wider for him. He slid his hand across her silken belly, searching for the wetness in which he wanted to be buried.

Inch by inch, Craig eased his finger into Shea's tightness, and he could tell that it had been a while since he had been with a man and it pleased him enormously. Another man wouldn't ever touch what was his after tonight.

Whimpering, Shea clawed at the sheets while he thrust his finger further inside her body. Her pussy sucked onto his finger like it was never going to let go. "Babe, you're such a nice tight fit for my finger. Will you be this snug for another part of me?"

"Yes...." She panted thrashing around on the bed.

That was what he wanted to hear. Easing his finger out of her body, Craig stood and slowly undressed as his gaze roamed over Shea's body. Shea had been built for loving, from her firm medium-sized breasts with their rock hard nipples, womanly stomach, fine hips, and shapely thighs. All of her was his to love and explore for as long as he wanted, and a lifetime was what he wanted.

Finding a stack of condoms in the drawer beside the bed, he quickly slipped one on.

"I'm so ready for you, too," he growled, easing completely between her welcoming thighs. He groaned and caught his breath as the heat of her caressed him. He hadn't even entered Shea yet, and she was already driving him mad.

Unable to wait any longer, he entered her with one sure, smooth thrust and almost passed out from the intense pleasure. If he had known Shea's body was this side of heaven he would have seduced her months ago.

"Your cock is so hot and thick," she cried, wrapping her legs around his back.

Short, sharp fingers scratched at his back while he slipped in and out of Shea's delicious warmth. He waited too long for this to happen to let it end early. Her body met his thrust for thrust, and there was nothing he could do she wasn't keeping up with.

He took and she gave. She took and he gave over and over until the he felt her body about to explode, but he couldn't let it until she promised him something.

"Promise me..." he said slowly down his thrusts.

"I'm so close, please don't stop," she begged, pulling at his hips.

"I know, baby, but promise me."

"Anything..."

"That you'll never leave me..." Craig rushed the words out as the tingling started in the base of his spine.

"I promise..." Shea screamed as the orgasm hit them both at the same time.

It shattered around them like a million fireworks on the Fourth of July, wiping out the last little part of himself that he hoped to keep hidden from Shea. Happiness bubbled into his veins as he withdrew from Shea and anchored her to his side.

"That was wonderful," she whispered, placing a kiss above his nipple, mindless to the sweat that covered both of their bodies. She fell asleep in his arms.

"It will only get better," Craig swore, and followed Shea into a blissful sleep.

Chapter Twenty-Three

"Baby, I need to go downstairs. I won't be gone that long," Craig whispered by her ear as he rolled out of bed, taking the warmth she loved so much with him.

Snuggling deeper into the firm mattress, Shea wrapped her satisfied body up in the comforter and peeked at Craig from underneath her lashes. She watched as he picked up his pants off the floor and slipped them on. Standing up, he looked down at her and a smile spread across his handsome face. Giving her a sexy 'bad boy' wink, he left the room, whistling the theme song to *The Andy Griffith Show*.

She waited until she heard the sounds of feet running down the stairs before she stretched out on the bed like a well-fed kitten. Her whole body was sore from making love, and she loved it. She had forgotten how good it felt to cut loose and let go. Craig took her to places that she had longed to remember but really hadn't missed until now. However, now she was addicted and wanted to visit them again and again.

Magic.

That was the only word she could use to describe the experience she felt with Craig all last night. Every time he reached for her she was there, ready to respond to him. He never got tired of touching her, and she never got tired of feeling his touch.

Hell, she couldn't keep this to herself. She had to call and tell Pierre about her night. For once in their friendship she had something juicy to tell her friend. Rolling over, Shea picked up the phone to punch in Pierre's cell phone number, but she heard Craig's voice on the other end. Not wanting to eavesdrop, she started to hang up until she heard him mention her name.

"Shea doesn't have a clue about that. How many times do I have to go over this with you?" Craig protested. "She isn't going to find out, either."

"I'm totally against you not telling her. She deserves to know the truth," Josh criticized in her ear. "She might not take it as hard as you think."

"Well, I'll never find that out, will I?" Craig tossed back.

"Secrets always have a way of resurfacing when you least expect it," Josh replied. "You have her now, so don't be afraid to confess this to her. It will be a huge weight off your shoulders."

"Okay, how am I supposed to confess to her?" Craig demanded. "Should it go something like this? Shea, I only asked you out on a date so I could get my hands on my aunt's stock. I knew with the crush you had on me that you would be easy pickings?"

Shea blinked back sudden tears and pressed her hand to her mouth so Craig and Josh wouldn't hear the sob that threatened to explode from her tight throat. Craig had used her. He was the bastard she first thought him to be, after all. Why hadn't she listened to that inner voice of hers?

Taking a deep breath, she tried to calm down blocking out the sound of her heart breaking into a million little pieces. Now wasn't the time to lose it completely and let Craig figure out that she was listening in on his discussion. Sinking her teeth into her bottom lip, she listened quietly as Craig continued his phone call with Josh.

"How about I confess the information Mr. Terry told me about weeks ago?" Craig asked. "Should I tell her about that, too, or wait until after she slaps me for withholding all my dirty secrets?"

"Don't yell at me," Josh shouted back. "It isn't my fault that the woman you love might hate you after all this is over."

"I don't love Shea," Craig said back to Josh, breaking the last piece of her heart.

Hot tears choked her as Shea slowly placed the phone back on the hook. She bolted from the bed. Hurrying around the room, she got dressed in record time and tossed her clothes inside her bag. She didn't care about the rest of them because she didn't want to see them again after tonight. Pain laced through her body, almost making it impossible to move, but she gathered her strength and searched the room for Craig's car keys. She finally found them inside the closet, in his coat pocket.

Squaring her shoulders, Shea opened the door and slipped out into the hallway, easing down the staircase. She sent out a silent prayer that Craig was in the family room and not the living room, so he wouldn't hear the car start.

She paused at the bottom step and listened as he joked around with Josh across the room. How could he be in there laughing having a good time when her heart was shattered? All the whispered words, slow lingering touches, and tender, passionate kisses had all been lies. The more she thought about it, the madder she became. She spun around to confront him.

Yet, halfway there she changed her mind and rushed from the house instead. She had to reach Mr. Terry first and find out the information Craig was hiding from her. That was more important than confronting the lying bastard inside the house.

Getting inside the car, Shea tossed her bag into the back seat and pulled out, praying Craig wouldn't notice she was gone until she was halfway back to town. She didn't feel an ounce of remorse for leaving his stranded out here by the lake. Maybe the time alone would give him some time to think about his sins.

As the car got further down the road, Shea took one last look in the rearview mirror and wished that things could have turned out differently for her and the man she loved.

* * * *

Shea hoped that the loud banging on Neil Terry's door would wake him up. She didn't care if he had to wipe the sleep from his eyes or the drool from his mouth. She wasn't leaving until he let her inside this building.

She stepped back from the door as the outside light was turned on above her head and Mr. Terry peeked out the vertical binds. He blinked at her a couple of times like he was surprised to see her at this time of night and then closed them. Blowing on her hands, she rubbed them together trying to keep them warm while she waited for him to open the door.

Miss Anderson, what are you doing out here in this weather?" Mr. Terry asked the second the door was opened.

"I came to find out Craig was supposed to tell me but didn't," she said, still rubbing her hands together.

"Come out to the back, Miss Anderson, and I'll get you a cup of hot chocolate. Then we can talk." He spun on his heel and left the room with Shea behind him.

Twenty minutes later, Shea sat working on her second cup of hot chocolate, wrapped up on an old blanket he found in his closet.

"Now let me start off by saying I don't think Craig purposely kept this from you, because I know that he had a lot going on when I told him about the clause in the will," Terry said.

"What clause?" she asked, blowing on her hot chocolate before taking a sip.

"The clause that states you have to sign the papers agreeing to accept the money and stocks from *Luscious Lips*, or all of them automatically go to Craig by default."

"That sneaky SOB," she hissed, slamming her cup down on the coffee table. "I knew all those words of love were lies."

"You shouldn't jump to conclusions, Miss Anderson. I'm sure Craig has a good explanation for not telling you about this sooner."

She dismissed his comment with a flick of her wrist. "No, you didn't hear what I heard tonight."

"What did you hear? You know not to pay attention to everything that comes out of Craig's mouth, don't you? Sometimes he says things before he thinks about them."

"No, he meant every word that came out of his mouth tonight, and I'm not about to forget it."

"You're too young to be so dramatic," he sighed. "I bet you'll be back with C.C. before the work week starts."

Shea glared at him, making a sudden chill come into the room and it had nothing to do with the weather outside. "I thought lawyers were supposed to be able to read people. Look into my eyes and tell me that I want Craig back in my life."

"Craig is in your blood. You won't be able to get rid of him that easily. The two of you are meant to be together. It's like you crave each other to a point of no return."

"I can get some medication prescribed for that," she said. "I'll move on with my life and so will he. Craig almost got what he wanted, so he'll be pissed for a few days, but he'll get over it."

"Why are young people are so pigheaded nowadays? I don't see how any of you ever get married and have a family," Neil complained. "Do you know why Rebecca gave you all the controlling interest in her company?"

Shea wrapped the plaid blanket tighter around her and shook her head. "I've been wondering about that for weeks now. Are you finally going to tell me the truth?" she asked. "I know she didn't think I could handle the responsibility of running a company that enormous."

"Shea, you're a very intelligent woman. I know you could have handled the everyday management of *Luscious Lips*. However, that isn't the entire reason Rebecca left it to you."

"It involves Craig, doesn't it?"

"Yes."

"Please don't tell me she was trying to play matchmaker with us. I told her I wasn't looking for a man in my life. I had other plans I wanted to accomplish first."

"Like owning your own bed and breakfast," he asked, and then grinned at Shea's shock.

"How do you know about that? Only one other person besides me knows about my B&B dream?"

"I wish I had a cool lawyer answer, but I don't. Rebecca saw you reading a book about it when you thought she was asleep."

"I can't believe it," Shea mused, tossing the blanket off her body. "I never knew she was awake when I was reading those books. She kept that to herself all that long."

"Rebecca thought if she left you the money it might bring you and C.C. closer together and then the sparks would fly."

"Sparks did fly, the day you read the will. I can still see the look on Craig's face when you were through. I'm surprised he didn't accuse me of killing her to get the money," Shea said under her breath.

"Craig wouldn't do anything like that to you," Neil quickly interjected, trying his best to smooth out whatever Shea heard Craig saying about her. "He cares a lot about you."

"I used to believe that until I heard him on the phone with Josh tonight," Shea said. "After hearing his opinion of me tonight, I don't want him or the money Rebecca left me."

"Please don't do something I might not be able to help you take back or fix," Terry said. "Craig wouldn't want you to do this either. Take a break and calm down. After you've had time to think you can talk things out with him."

Leaning forward, Shea rested her elbows on her legs and plastered a hard look on her face. "No, my mind is made up. I don't want the stocks anymore. Give me the papers to sign that will give everything to Craig. I was doing well before him, and I'll be doing even better after he's gone."

"Are you sure about this? You still have some time to think this over," he suggested. "After the papers are signed and filed you won't be able to get the money back from Craig."

"I'm a hundred percent positive that I don't want anything that is attached to Craig Clark Evans. So, please stop asking me and go get those papers."

Neil left the room and came back several papers were inside his hand. "Are you really sure about this? You still have until Thanksgiving, that is the deadline Rebecca gave you." Coming back over to his desk, he took his seat. "Rebecca wanted you to have this money for help with your dream. She wouldn't want you to allow Craig's indifference to ruin that for you."

"No, I want him to keep it because it's his family's money, not mine," she said, reaching for a pen. "Show me where to sign so I can get this over with."

Neil took one last look into Shea' eyes and seemed to realized she was closed to his suggestions, and that it would be a waste of his breath to argue anymore with her. He quickly flipped open the folder and pointed to a line at the bottom of the page. "Sign here and I'll take care of the rest."

Sadness mixed with a dash of anger settled in the middle of her chest as Shea signed away her dreams for a man she thought had loved her. "How long will it take you to file the papers and for Craig to get the money?" Shea asked. "I don't want him bothering me about this. He got what he plotted for, so he should be a very elated man."

"With the holiday coming up I won't file them until the following week. I don't want them to get lost in the shuffle."

"Well, I can't do anything about that, but can you do a favor for me?"

"Name it."

"Can you give me a ride home? I drove Craig's rental car here and I don't want him coming to the house to pick it up."

"I wish that I could, but my wife drove me here because I wanted to work late. Our other car is in the shop and she's probably at home sound asleep. However, I can call a cab for you," Neil replied. "I'll also contact Craig about the car. I know the people he rented the cottage from."

"Thank you, I would love for you to do that. He has probably reported it stolen by now."

"How about I call that cab for you and get you another cup of hot chocolate? It will take a while for it to come way out here. Plus I'm going to pay for it and I don't want to hear you say no," Neil said the second Shea opened her mouth.

"Thank you so much, Mr. Terry." Shea gave him a small smile.

"Not a problem that's what I'm here for," he replied softly.

Chapter Twenty-Four

"You have to know where she is, for God's sake, you're her best friend," Craig barked into the phone. He had come back upstairs after his phone call with Josh and found Shea, then his car, gone. How could she up and leave him alone like this, especially after the night they shared and the promise she made?

"Listen, Craig, I don't know where she is. Shea was supposed to be spending a relaxing weekend with you. What did you do to her? Did you yell at her after she told you she wanted to spend some of the money on a bed and breakfast?" Pierre snapped.

Bed and breakfast?

"Pierre, I don't know what you're talking about. Shea hasn't mentioned that to me." He thought it was wonderful his woman wanted her own career. Hell, he'd be happy to help her anyway he could. Shea was way too smart to stay at the insurance company the rest of her life.

"Furthermore, I would never yell at Shea. I'm in love with her. Are you sure she hasn't gotten in touch with you?" He was growing more worried by the minute. Something must have happened for her to up and leave like she did, but he didn't know what it was.

"Do you think she got a phone call from her family on her cell phone and that's why she left me without saying goodbye? I would have gotten dressed and went with her."

"TMI," Pierre sighed on the other end of the line.

"What in the hell does TMI mean?" He was wasting time listening to Pierre talk in code.

"It's something my niece would say. It means *too much information,* and I don't believe anything is wrong with her family. I haven't gotten any phone calls. Our mothers are best friends, so I would know if something was."

"Fine," he snapped. "How about you tell me then why the woman I want to marry and start a family with left me? Was I that bad of a lover that she couldn't face me in the morning?"

"Once again, Craig, TMI," Pierre complained. "I don't need to hear all of that, but I do have a question."

"Shoot."

"What were you talking to Josh about on the phone? Was it something that Shea could have overheard and got upset about? I was waiting for her phone call myself, but she never called me."

Icy fear twisted around his heart as Craig collapsed on the bed behind him. Panic like he had never experienced before welled up in the center of his chest. "What time did Shea say she would call you tonight?"

Pierre paused on her end of the phone while she thought about his question. "If I'm guessing right I think it was around seven o'clock because it's always before I take my dog for a walk."

No, he wouldn't let those thoughts enter his mind. His luck wasn't that bad. Fate didn't have it out for him. Craig tried to make his heart believe what his mind was trying to tell him, but he knew what the answer was.

"Pierre, I've to go. Thanks for all your help," he whispered, then hung up the phone. *Please God, don't let it be true*. But he knew it was.

Shea had heard him on the phone and left without giving him time to explain. He would bet his last dollar on it. Why had he let Josh get him into that same old tired conversation again? Josh loved yanking his chain sometimes, and this time it had cost him the most important person in his life. Well, he wouldn't let it happen. He would find Shea and make her listen to him.

His blood pounded at the thought of Shea completely shutting him out of her life. A lot of emotions were coursing through his body, yet the biggest one was a deep shame over the thought of using Shea even crossed his mind in the first place.

He was frantic to find her and let her know what she heard wasn't the truth. He wasn't dating her to get his aunt's stock back. Hell, she could keep them or sell them for all he cared. All he ever needed was her to be in his life. A part of him suspected that his aunt set this whole will thing up just to bring the two of them together. Now, he allowed his big mouth to open and ruin the most fantastic time of his life.

"Shit, I'm about to lose Shea over a stupid conversation she overheard on the phone. I'm going to find her and lock both of us up in a room. We'll stay there until she understands I'm in love with her and always have been."

His plan was perfect, but he had one little problem standing in his way of true happiness. Where in the hell had Shea gone if she wasn't with Pierre? He knew that she wouldn't go and see Josh.

"Think," he said, tapping the side of his head with his finger. "Shea doesn't socialize with that many people, so whom would she go to, and at this time of night?" Craig racked his mind until he started feeling a headache.

"Please, just give me a hint of where she is and I'll take it from there," he pleaded inside the empty room.

Two seconds after his plea left his mouth, the phone on the night table rung behind him. Craig rushed back over to it and jerked it up to his ear, "Shea, is that you? We need to talk."

"No, it isn't Shea," Mr. Terry snapped in his ear.

"Just leave it I have to call you back. Shea is gone and I need to find her. I'll call you back after I make sure she's okay." He started to disconnect the call, but Mr. Terry's harsh voice stopped him.

"Craig, Shea isn't missing. I was with her less than an hour ago waiting for a cab to come pick her up. I'm madder than hell at you. How could you do that to her? She's such a sweet young woman."

"I haven't done anything to her," Craig denied. "Shea up and left me while I was downstairs on the phone with Josh. Do you know the panic I felt when I came upstairs and found her gone? Tell me where she is. I need to talk to her," he pleaded.

"She doesn't want to see or hear from you. I only called to let you know two things. Your rental car is at my office, so you need to find a way to pick it up; and congratulations, you finally got what you wanted."

Congratulations?

Why was Mr. Terry talking in riddles? Time was wasting. The longer Shea stayed away from him, the more she would rebuild the wall around her heart. He had to get Neil to tell him where Shea was so he could go to her. "What are the congratulations for?"

"You have to ask after everything you did to get it?"

"Look, I don't have time for this. Spit it out and then tell me where Shea is," Craig demanded.

"You are the sole owner of *Luscious Lips*. Shea signed over all her stocks to you. I've never seen a woman so brokenhearted in my life."

Misery was like a steel weight on his shoulders as raw guilt tore at him. No, this couldn't be happening to him, not now. He just found Shea, he wasn't about to lose her.

"Shea needed that money. She wanted to start her own business and she doesn't have that kind of capital. Neil, tell me where she is so I can shake some sense into her," he pleaded. "Also, don't file those papers. I don't want *Luscious Lips*. It belongs to Shea. I'm in love with her. I can't let her slip out of my life."

"I don't know," Mr. Terry paused. "When she left my office I don't think she wanted to hear from you."

"I'm desperate, please help me," Craig begged, counting the ways he had ruined the love Shea had shown him. "Man, I love her. Don't you understand what I'm telling you?"

"I watched her get into a cab, trying her best not to break down. I know she was going home, but I don't know if she still there or not. Craig, she's really hurting. Don't rush over there and bulldoze her. Be kind to her feelings and listen to her side first."

"How do you know so much about a woman's feelings?"

"I haven't been married for twenty-seven years for nothing," Mr. Terry replied. "Remember my advice, but more importantly take it."

"I will," he promised, then hung up the phone.

Picking it back up, he called Josh, "I need you to come out to the cottage and pick me up. Shea heard me when I was on the phone with you and left with the rental car.

Chapter Twenty-Five

Dear Journal,

Why didn't you tell me not to fall in love with Craig? I shouldn't have let my damn emotions rule me. How many times did I wonder were his feelings genuine? Too many to count on both hands, and I know I should still be upset, but my crying days are over. I'm pissed that he used me like this.

I gave him everything I had, and he made fun of me with Josh. How many times had he done it without me knowing? Tonight wasn't the first time he discussed me with his buddy. However, it is the last. I'm through with Craig Clark Evans. I deserve better than what he has to offer me.

Thanksgiving is coming up, so I might not be able to write in you until after it's over. I can't believe I thought about inviting him to spend Thanksgiving with my family. I'm so glad he showed his true colors first.

Closing the book with a snap, Shea slid it back into its familiar spot by the bed. Shea closed her eyes and listen to the wind blowing outside. In Maine, November was the beginning of winter and she hated it. It seemed like the daylight didn't last as long, and by the end of the month it would be freezing.

Storms sometimes increased, too, during this month, but she prayed that it would pass over this year. Last year Maine was hit with too many storms for her taste, making it was too wet and uncomfortable.

What happened to her life? God, less than twenty-four hours ago she was making love to the man she was in love with, and now she was thinking about the weather. She tried not to feel disappointed that Craig hadn't even tried to get in contact with her. She knew Mr. Terry had gotten in touch with him by now about the will, but he must not have cared.

"Shea, I know you're in there. I need to talk with you," a voice yelled up at her window, scaring the hell out of her.

Jumping up off the bed, she rushed over to the window and pulled back the curtains. Craig stood below, looking gorgeous in all black with his hair brushed back from his face.

No, calm down. Don't fall for his look. Stay strong.

Raising up the window, she flinched as a blast of cold air hit her in the face, "No, I don't have anything to say to you. Now go home and leave me the hell alone."

"Not a chance, gorgeous. You made a promise to me and I expect you to keep it," Craig shouted up at her.

"I made that promise before I found out what a lying asshole you are," Shea screamed down at the man who still had a piece of her heart.

"Fine, I'm an asshole. I'll admit to that, but you have to know that I love you," Craig insisted.

She had to control the urge not to throw something out the window at Craig's head. "You only loved what I had and now it's gone, so I'm finished with you. Go away and don't come back here. I'm going to find a man who loves me for myself."

"The hell you will! You're mine and another man won't ever touch you," Craig hollered. "Don't do this, Shea. Come downstairs and let me in," his voice dropped lower, more soothing. "We don't have to do anything but talk. I swear I'll listen to you."

"Craig, it's cold and I'm tired. Go home before one of my neighbors calls the police on you."

"If I have to go to jail to prove my love for you, I'll do it."

Shea took a deep breath and forbade herself to tremble or get excited about Craig's words. They were all lies and she knew it now. Taking one long last lingering look at the man standing on her grass, she whispered, "Goodbye, Craig."

Moving back, she shut the window and locked it, and then closed the curtains. Shea went over to the CD player on the dresser and pushed play. Jody Watley's voice filled her bedroom, blocking out Craig's tortured voice from outside.

* * * *

"Fuck!" Craig howled as he stood outside staring up at Shea's closed bedroom. He knew he should have come straight over here instead of changing clothes like Josh suggested. She wouldn't have cared if he showed up wearing the same clothes. She only wanted to hear that he loved her.

Now she was beyond pissed and nothing he said tonight was going to change that. His mouth might have finally dug a hole that he might not be able to crawl out of. But he had to get Shea back

Craig shoved his hands into the pockets of his leather jacket, feeling the cold settling into his body, yet he didn't want to leave. Shea was in pain and he was the only person that could heal it. Consequently, she wasn't about to let him within twenty feet of her.

"Shea, I'll be back tomorrow and I'm not leaving until I talk to you," he hollered up at the window. Craig took one last look at the house he urgently wanted to be in, then he got into his car and left.

Chapter Twenty-Six

Padding around in the kitchen with a thick pair of wool socks on her feet, Shea turned over the bacon in the skillet and started the coffeemaker. She wasn't worry about her weight today, she needed her comfort food.

The aroma brought back memories of when her mother woke up earlier and fixed breakfast for her and her siblings. It was the best time for all of them. On special days each one of them got to be responsible for one item on the table.

Virginia always got to flip over the pancakes, she got the bacon, and Taymar got to pour the orange juice. Sometimes she missed being at home and having her mother to confide in about her problems. She called her at least once a week to check in, but it wasn't the same.

Taking the bacon out of the skillet, she placed it on a paper towel covered plate and set it to the side. She was headed to the table for her coffee mug when the doorbell rung and stopped her.

"It better not be Craig, or he'll get the door slammed back in his face," she said, making her way to the front door. She glanced through the peephole and screamed. Opening the door, she flung her body against the man standing on the other side.

"What in the world are you doing here?" she asked, stepping back.

"I came for a visit. I hope that's okay," he grinned as his coal black eyes shined down into hers.

"You know it is. Come on in here and get out of the cold. Can't have you catching a cold," she replied, waving her visitor inside. "I'm working on breakfast, do you want some?"

"When have I ever turned down your cooking?" Her guest laughed, shoving her back into the house and slamming the door closed behind them.

* * * *

A lone figure grew colder than the weather outside as he watched the door slam shut behind Shea and the man she dragged inside her house. Looking down at the envelope in his hand, Craig tossed it into the passenger seat beside him.

"I can't believe she jumped into the arms of another man so quickly after me. She never came off as a slut to me. Guess I was wrong about her. Glad I didn't make the mistake of popping the question like I wanted."

Craig sat inside his car a little longer and imagined what the two of them were doing together. "Damn it, she's in there having sex with another man and I'm out here in the cold worrying about it. I'm done with her. I don't need that gutter trash in my life," he complained as he drove off in a huff, not wanting to admit his true feelings.

* * * *

"How long are you planning on hiding here at my place?"

"As long as it takes to make her realize I'm not a child," Taymar complained, reaching for another slice of bacon and two pieces of toast.

"You aren't acting like an adult, and you know this is the first place she'll call."

"Aren't big sisters supposed to protect their baby brothers?" Taymar took a bite of his cinnamon toast.

"Virginia is your big sister, too, and her house is bigger than mine," Shea lectured, pouring her spoiled little brother some more orange juice.

"Are you crazy? She's worse than Mom," he choked out over the toast in his mouth. "You're the cool one. Can I stay?"

"Only on two conditions," Shea answered, getting up from the table with her empty plate in hand. She stuck the plate into the soapy dishwater, then faced Taymar.

"What are they?" Taymar asked, getting up with his empty plate. Reaching around her, he shoved it into the dishwater.

"First condition, you have to call Mama and let her know that you're here. Second condition, you have to leave by the middle of next month. I'm not going to baby sit you while you figure out your life."

Taymar gave her his typical baby brother groan. "Sis, can't I stay at least still the first of the year? Monica is driving me crazy about the baby. I can't handle all the pressure."

"No, you made your little boy and you need to be a father to him," she said. "Plus you have school. I'm not going to let you get kicked out for missing too many days."

"I'll be a father to my son. I'm only asking for a break for a little bit." Taymar sighed. "Anyways I'm smart. I can transfer here and finish out my senior year."

"I'm giving you a break by letting you stay here in the first place, and didn't I send you the money to help with the hospital bills?"

"Thanks for that. I didn't know how I was going to pay for them," Taymar replied. "I'll agree to your conditions. Why don't you go upstairs and get dressed? I can finish these dishes, and when you come back down you can tell me about your boyfriend."

Shea froze at the sink and shook off the memory of Craig outside her window last night. *Keep him in the past.* "I don't have a boyfriend," she corrected, brushing past her baby brother. She hated when he acted like he was older than her.

"Yes, you do. I heard Mom telling one of her bingo friends about him the other night. When are you going to bring him home to meet the family? You know Dad is ready to meet him."

"I told you I don't have a boyfriend. Stop drilling me about him and finish those dishes," she tossed back as she hurried from the kitchen. The sound of her brother's laughter followed her all the way upstairs.

* * * *

He stood on Shea's porch for almost two minutes before finally deciding to ring the doorbell. Craig didn't know why he came back here, but he just knew he had to see his replacement up close.

187

Keep your cool. No matter what happens don't let him get the best of you. Say your peace and walk away. There are other women out there waiting for you. Craig repeated that several times in his mind as he waited for someone to answer the door.

"Yeah, can I help you?" the guy that Shea hugged asked the second the front door opened.

He's younger than me. Craig stared at the young man blocking the entranceway into Shea's house. If he was to guess, the guy couldn't be older than twenty-one years old. He never thought of Shea as a cradle-robber. How long had she been seeing this guy?

"I need to speak to Shea," Craig responded once he got his voice back.

Jet black eyes narrowed on his face. "She's upstairs in the shower. Can I ask who you are?"

Gut wrenching pain raced through his body, almost making it hard for him to stand up, Shea had slept with this college jock, and now was upstairs taking a shower. How could she do this to them?

Disgust laced his words. "No, you can't ask who I am. But I'll give you a piece of advice. Shea is a damn good lay, but once you cross her she'll jump into bed with the next available guy. So, I'll be careful if I were you. You're young, don't let her play you. Dump her and find a girl closer to your own age."

Out of nowhere a hard punch hit him right below the eye, staggering him back from the door. "You son of a bitch. Who in the hell do you think you are to talk about Shea like that? She isn't a slut!" the guy yelled, then took another menacing step towards him.

He shook off the ringing his ear and stormed back up to the younger guy. "You may have surprised me once, but I won't let you sucker punch me again. I'll give as good as I get. Are you sure Shea is worth fighting over?"

"Hell, yes!" came the heated reply.

Craig was ready to go another around with the mystery guy when a flash of burgundy stepped between the two of them, "What in the hell is going on out there? I can hear the two of you upstairs in my bedroom," Shea yelled, shoving him away from her new lover.

"I was just telling your new boy toy here what a great lay you were and he got all pissed off," he snapped, brushing Shea's hand off his chest.

"Stop talking about Shea like that or I'll punch the hell out of you again," the younger man screamed, lunging for him.

Spinning away from him, Shea pushed his replacement back toward the front door. "Go inside the house and make that phone call. I'll deal with this."

"I'm not leaving you out here with him!"

"Taymar, go and do as I'll ask," Shea shouted.

"Fine, I'll go, but I'll be watching you through the window," the younger guy promised, then went back into the house, slamming the door.

"I didn't know you like them manageable with milk still on their breath," Craig snickered above Shea's head.

"Why are you here? I thought we settled this last night. It's over between us," Shea replied, fixing him with those dark eyes he still loved so much.

"I came by this morning to talk things through with you and that's when I saw you with lover boy at your door. I left and then came back to confront him. He hit me, and that's when you came out."

"Did you ask Taymar who he was before you tossed out your low opinion of me?" she whispered.

"Why did I have to ask who he was? I saw with my own two eyes how you embraced him. You only hug a man like that if you love him. Do you love him?" Craig held his breath while he waited for an answer.

Shaking her head, Shea looked up at him with sad eyes. "Yes, I love him. I've loved him most of my life."

Wanting her to feel the same hurt as him, Craig lashed out at Shea, "Fine, love him all you want, but when he gets tired of you don't run back to me. I don't take back damaged goods."

"Craig, listen to me and listen good because I'm not going to say this again. You've hurt me for the last time with your careless words. After today I don't want to see you, or hear from you. I'm moving on with my life and I suggest you do the same thing."

The hurt look Shea gave him touched the deepest part of his soul. "We could have been good together, but you ruined it. Goodbye for good, Craig." Turning on her heel, Shea strolled back into the house and closed the door softly behind her, leaving him alone in the cold.

Chapter Twenty-Seven

"Sis, I think it's so cool that you want to open your own bed and breakfast, but you need to get out of the house. The only thing you do is go to work and come home. You can't allow Craig to keep you locked away in the house," Taymar complained, grabbing the notebook out of her hand. "Let me take you out to dinner."

Snatching the notebook back, Shea glared at her brother. "You don't have any money. How can you take me out to dinner? Besides, I need to finish researching."

"Researching what?"

"All sort of things, from how I want the lobby to be set up: adults only, or families with children or pets. I need to check into reservation services, booking agencies, tourist information centers. What about word or mouth or private advertising? This is a big responsibility I'm jumping into and I want everything to be perfect. I can't let one thing go wrong or it might ruin everything," she sighed.

"Shea, you're one of the smartest women I know and you'll do an excellent job. I only want to take you out for a few hours to get you over your asshole ex-boyfriend. Isn't that what baby brothers are for?

Besides, dad gave me a credit card for emergencies and I think this qualifies as one."

"I'll make a deal with you. Give me have an hour to finish working on my notes and I'll let you take me out to dinner."

"Great, I'll call Monica and see how she is doing." Taymar hugged her, then got up from the couch. "Hey, why don't I call Pierre and invite her along, too? She's always the life of the party, and I haven't seen her since the last time I was in town."

"Do you still have a crush on her?"

"No," Taymar denied a little too quickly. "I wanted her around to lift up your spirits."

She didn't say a word, but she thought her baby brother still had a crush on her friend. "Pierre's phone number is in my address book by the bed. Try her cell phone first, and then if you don't get her try the work number."

"Sure thing," Taymar grinned, then raced up the stairs, leaving her alone.

* * * *

Owning your own Bed and Breakfast: advantages and disadvantages

Advantages
1. Be your own boss
2. Earn extra money
3. Work at home
4. Continue other interests
5. Meet new people
6. Choose your customers

Disadvantages

1. Less privacy
2. Work load
3. Maybe some income loss

Shea checked over the list one more time to make sure she wasn't forgetting anything. Taymar didn't know what he was talking about. She wasn't hiding in the house from Craig. He was part of her past. It didn't matter that he left a burning imprint on her.

How could he think she would jump from his bed to another man's in less than twenty four hours? His ex-girlfriends might lead that kind of lifestyle, but she didn't. Hell, Craig was only the third man she had ever slept with.

"Stop allowing him to control your thoughts. I have a career to get on the road now, and I need all of my attention for that." Vowing to forget about Craig and how she was secretly still in love with him, Shea continued working on her list.

* * * *

"Have you heard anything back from the bank yet?" Pierre asked, sipping at her mixed drink. "I still think was a mistake that you signed all the money back over to that self-centered asshole. Rebecca left it to you. She loved you and wanted you to have it."

"I had to break all ties with him. I loved Rebecca, too, but Craig would have always been breathing down my neck for the money, so I gave it to him. No, I haven't heard from the bank. They said they would get back in touch with me before Thanksgiving."

"Thanksgiving is next week," Taymar cut in. "Are you going back home with me? Mom and Dad wanted to see you."

"Yea, I'm going back. Being around the entire family will be nice, and I need to get out of town," Shea answered. "I'm praying the bank will call before I leave, but you never know."

"Well, if you want to hear my two cents, I think you'll be perfect for a B&B," Pierre said. "You're friendly, tolerant, hospitable, and motivated and a hard worker."

"Don't forget about organized, and a neat freak," Taymar added.

"Thanks, guys, for making me sound as dull as watching paint dry," Shea sighed, watching couples going in and out of the restaurant. She gasped when a familiar face walked through the door. "Great, I don't have time to deal with him. If you'll excuse me, I need to go to the ladies room." She got up and left the table, leaving Pierre and her brother staring after her confused.

* * * *

"Do you know why Shea up and left like that?" Taymar asked, reaching for the last roll inside the basket.

"I don't know," Pierre answered, still looking in the direction her friend disappeared in. She was very worried about Shea. She was working way too many hours at the insurance agency, and when she wasn't there her time was spent on getting the B&B things together.

"How's the sexiest woman in the room?" a voice whispered behind her.

Pierre twisted her head and connected eyes with Josh. Now she knew why Shea had made a mad dash for the restroom.

Josh wouldn't leave her alone. He had asked her out on three different occasions, and her snappy attitude wasn't running him off. It was kind of a turn-on the way he kept showing up and flirting with her.

"I'm fine."

"You sure are," Josh agreed, taking Shea's seat. "Who's your date?" he asked, a hint of envy and curiosity in his voice. "He seems a little young for you."

"Taymar isn't my date. He's Shea's baby brother. We all decided to have a late dinner together," she answered. "Why are you here?"

"I'm here to pick up some takeout. Craig and I are working late."

"You tell that punk to stay away from my sister," Taymar snapped at him as his lanky frame rose from the table. "Tell Shea I went outside to smoke and I'll be back in a minute."

Josh stared at Taymar's retreating form, then back at her, "What his problem?"

Her brow furrowed as she stared at Josh. "Are you telling me Craig didn't tell you about the fight he had with Taymar the other day?"

"Craig mentioned he confronted some guy that Shea was sleeping with…" Josh's mouth fell open as it dawned on him. "Don't tell me Taymar was the guy?"

"Yes, and it tore Shea up. She was hurt, pissed, and crushed all at the same time," Pierre snapped.

She had never seen her best friend so angry and she had every reason to be.

"Why didn't she tell him who Taymar was?"

"Craig never gave her a chance. He did what he always does, placed blame and stormed off. Are you implying that Shea is the wrong one here?"

Josh held up his hands in mock surrender. "I'm not defending Craig or blaming Shea. I think it was just a situation that got out of hand. Like her overhearing the phone call that broke them up in the first place," he answered.

"Don't get me started on that damn phone call, either. How dare you pretend to be innocent? You were a part of it, too."

"Listen, I don't want us to get into the middle of this. Craig and Shea are meant to be together and they will work through this. I only want to focus on us and whether or not I can take you out on a date."

Pierre hated how much she wanted to say yes, but it wasn't going to happen as long as Shea was still upset at Craig. "I'll say yes to you when I'm the maid of honor at Craig and Shea's wedding and not a day before."

If she expected Josh to be taken back, she got the surprise of her life. He grinned at her like he knew a secret. "Not a problem. I'll ask you out again the day of the wedding." Winking at her, Josh got up from the table, leaving behind a small hint of his cologne behind to tempt her.

Sitting at the table, Pierre was lost in a trance. Josh honestly thought Shea and Craig would be back together. She shrugged her shoulders and took another sip of her drink. "Well, if it happens I'll keep my end of the deal," she said out loud.

"What deal are you talking about?" Shea asked, rejoining her at the table. "What did Josh want? I didn't think the two of you liked each other because I know he wasn't over here asking about me."

"You would be surprised what Josh wanted," Pierre replied. "Let me order you a drink and I'll fill you in." Raising her hand, she waved a waitress back over to their table and proceeded to tell Shea about her odd conversation with Josh.

Chapter Twenty-Eight

"I thought you had gotten lost with our food or something," Craig complained, clearing off the table so Josh could take the Chinese food out of the bag. "What took you so long anyway?"

Josh laid out all the containers of food—chicken egg rolls, beef lo mein, barbecued pork, and fried rice with shrimp—and then sat down at the table. "I saw Pierre and I stopped to talk to her."

Craig hated to ask, but he couldn't help himself. It had been almost a week since he talked to Shea, and he missed the hell out of her. Several times he thought about going back to her house and telling her new guy to get lost. "Did you see Shea there?"

"No, I didn't see Shea there, but later on I found out that she was there," Josh answered, dishing himself a nice helping of the popped rice with shrimp. "However, I did run into the young man you had a fight with. I found out something very interesting about him, too."

Handing Josh a paper towel and some utensils, Craig joined him at the table. "I can't believe you actually got the barbecued pork. I can never get it when I go there." He scooped out two spoonfuls. "I don't want to hear about Shea's new young stud, either. Whatever you found out you can keep it to yourself. I want to eat my food in peace. Shea is gone from my life and I couldn't be happier," he lied, not wanting to admit how much he still missed Shea.

Josh waved his fork in his direction. "I think you might want to hear this. His name is Taymar and he's…"

"Didn't I tell you to keep it to yourself?" Craig snapped. "I already know who he is."

"C.C., I really need to tell you this."

"Shut up and eat your food. We still have to finish up the PowerPoint and run through it one last time. I don't want to be here all night. Sherri is expecting me at her house tonight." He ignored how Josh glowered at him.

"You can't be serious. How can you be going out with her? Damn it, Craig when are you going to stop acting like an asshole and admit that Shea is the only woman for you?"

"I did tell Shea that I loved her," Craig exploded, "and you know what she did? She left me after she promised that she never would and ran into the arms of another man…no, a boy. How do you think I felt watching her open her front door and run into his arms like he was her world? I sat outside in my car and watched *my* world crumble around me. I wanted to make her my wife but she betrayed me. I won't stand by and wait for something that isn't meant to be."

"Is that how your mind really works?" Josh asked. "Shea never betrayed you. She was totally in love with you from the first moment she laid eyes on you. Everyone in town knew it, and I was always dumbfounded by the fact that you didn't. You told me over the phone that you *didn't* love her and she heard you. Why are you trying to blame her for a mistake you made? Yes, if she had stuck around she would have heard you say that you were in love with her, and how she made the hole in your heart finally complete, but she never listened to those words. So, now it's up to you to find a way to make her."

Craig was starting to get fed up with Josh and all his happily-ever-after advice. When would it finally sink in his head that Shea tossed him away, not the other way around? Getting rejected wasn't something he was used to, and he didn't want to open up his heart again to another blow.

"I'm not dating Sherri. She needs me to help her with her cover art for her next book. I'm not that low to crawl into another woman's bed. Shit, I'm still in love with Shea."

"That's fantastic, "Josh grinned, reaching for the beef lo mein. "You can apologize to her again and the both of you should be back together before Thanksgiving."

Craig rubbed his hand across his the back of his neck. Something was wrong with Josh's hearing or he was suffering a chemical imbalance of the brain because he wasn't getting it through his head about Shea and her new man. "What about this Taymar? Will he just step to the side and let me waltz away with Shea?" he taunted.

"Well, he was still pretty pissed when I brought your name up at the table with Pierre. But I think if you apologize for calling his sister a slut he might forgive you."

The bottom of Craig's stomach dropped out, rolled across the floor, and crawled into the trashcan. "What did you say?" he said.

As cockily as he could be, Josh laid his fork next to his plate and gave him a deadpan stare. "In your hurry to punish Shea for not keeping her promise, you accused her of sleeping with her own brother."

That guy was her brother?

"No, I don't believe you." He wouldn't have made that huge of a mistake.

"Pierre would have no reason to lie, and neither would Taymar."

"Josh, what have I done?" Craig groaned, shoving his full plate away. The scent of the food was making him sick. "I've got to get her back. What do you think, flowers, candy, stuffed animals, me down on my hands and knees begging for her forgiveness? I'll take any advice you want to give me."

"Buddy, I don't know. I've never been in a relationship long enough to want to apologize to a woman. Furthermore, I never loved a woman the way you do Shea. But you better do it quickly or you'll be spending Thanksgiving alone."

"I know, but I'll pray I haven't killed all the love she had for me. I'd love to spend Thanksgiving with her, but I'll miss that to have a lifetime with her."

Getting up from the table, Josh picked up the container of chicken egg rolls. "I'm going to finish my dinner in my office and leave you in here alone to think. I hope you can figure out a way to win Shea back." With that said, Josh turned away from him went out the door, shutting it softly behind him.

"So do I," Craig sighed.

Chapter Twenty-Nine

"Shea, what are you doing you doing in this part of town?" a sinful, sexy voice questioned behind her. She trembled at her name on those firm lips again and hoped he hadn't noticed. "Aren't you usually at work this time of day?"

Twirling around, she stared up at Craig almost lost the control she was trying so hard to keep. She hadn't laid eyes on him for over a week, and he was looking so damn fine. His hair seemed longer and the caramel-colored jacket strained against the muscles she got to touch that one time they made love at the cottage. A Kelly green sweater brought out the greenish flecks in his eyes.

"I'm here registering my name for the B&B I'm trying to get started," she replied, sliding her hands into her pockets so she wouldn't touch him.

"Yeah, I heard about that," Craig answered, moving towards her. "Do you have a few minutes so we can talk? I want…need to tell you something."

"No. I don't have any extra time to talk," she retorted, backing away. "I have to get home and pack. I'm going home for Thanksgiving."

"Shea, I know now that Taymar is your brother, and I apologize for all the nasty things I said to you.

Can't we spend Thanksgiving together and work through this? Baby, I still love you."

Craig slipped his hands through her hair and rested his forehead against hers. "Please stay here with me."

Shea wanted to say yes so bad, but the pain of his words were still fresh and deep. She couldn't let him off that easily, and her family was counting on her to show up. She laid her hands on Craig's butter soft jacket and eased back from him. "I can't." Spinning away, she hurried down the sidewalk, blending into the crowd.

* * * *

"Princess, why are you sitting all alone here in the dark?" Raymond Anderson asked, taking a seat next to his daughter. "You didn't eat that much Thanksgiving dinner, and your mother made that chess pie especially for you."

"I wasn't really that hungry, Daddy." She stared out the window at the swing hanging in the backyard. It looked the same as it did when she was a little girl.

"Are you thinking about Craig?"

Her head swung around, meeting a keen pair of light brown eyes in an almost wrinkle free face except for the slight crow's feet around the eyes. "How do you know about him? Did Mama tell you?"

"No, your brother did, and from what I heard I don't think I'd like this young man. How dare he call you those names? He better not let me see his face or I'll knock some sense into him."

Raymond Anderson had been a boxer for almost thirty-five years of his life, but quit when he met her mother. Shea knew her dad could hurt Craig and she didn't want that to happen. "Daddy, you don't have to worry about that. I'm not dating him anymore."

"Well, he's a fool not to know what a treasure he had in my little princess." He father kissed her on the top of her head. "But I can hear it in your voice, you're still in love with him, aren't you?"

Shea opened her mouth to deny it until a finger waved in front of her face. "Don't you lie to me, Shea."

"Yes, Daddy, I do and I hate it," Shea confessed. "Craig can be so controlling sometimes, but the times when he looked at me like I was the center of his world did me in."

"He's in love with you, too." The words were a statement and not a question.

"What makes you say that after the way he talked to me? I thought you wanted to punch his face in. Now you're taking up for him."

Burly arms wrapped around her and the memories of her childhood engulfed her. "Princess, men will say and do a lot of things when they are in love with a woman. Lashing out is the first thing that happens, especially when he's jealous. I wanted to be mad at Craig, but the second you said his name this soft sound came into your voice. He's the one and you know it."

Leaning back, she stared into her father's face. "Are you saying I should go to him and take him back?"

"You're an Anderson. We don't seek out or give an apology. We have the apology given to us," her father corrected, placing her head back on his chest.

"Now, let's sit here a few more minutes and then we can head back in the kitchen and get a piece of pie."

"With ice cream?" Shea asked.

"Two scoops," her father laughed.

* * * *

The microwave went off and a pair of hands pulled out the turkey with dressing, mashed potatoes, and peas. Thanksgiving TV dinner. Closing the door with his elbow, Craig took the meal over to the table and dropped it down. This wasn't how he envisioned spending his Thanksgiving, working late on a project for Josh while his buddy went home to spend the holiday with his family, then coming home to a tasteless meal.

Falling into the chair, Craig dug into the potatoes and cringed at the bland taste. Picking up his napkin, he spit them out and tossed the napkin on top of the TV dinner, then shoved both of them away.

"I'm supposed to be with Shea today, not alone. Why did I ever think *Luscious Lips* was more important than her? I've got the stock and nothing else. Aunt Rebecca set it up so Shea and I would be together by now, and I totally ruined her final wishes.

"Aunt Rebecca, please help me find a way to win back Shea. I thought I might have gotten through to her but she ran from me. I don't want to talk about the pain that caused me. I swear if I get another chance I won't ruin it."

Craig brushed his hair off his forehead and got up from the table. This was the worst Thanksgiving he had ever had, and he couldn't wait until tomorrow. Shea was probably taking a long weekend to be with her family. So, he didn't count on her being back until Tuesday at the latest. When she got back he was going to approach her again and make her realize was the man for her.

"I won't spend another holiday without Shea and my ring on her finger."

Chapter Thirty

Dear Journal.

I don't know what I'm going to do. I've been back in town for two days and everywhere I turn I see Craig. How can I work through my emotions for Craig? He has sent me flowers, an adorable stuffed baby Sylvester (how he knew I like that cartoon I'll never know) and yesterday he even paid for my coffee. I can't take this.

"I didn't know you still wrote in that thing," Pierre said, joining her at the table. "I should start one, but I'll never have the patience to keep it going. I'll be bored after only one entry."

"Writing helps calm me down." Snapping the journal shut, Shea dropped it into her purse beside her chair. "Now tell me the good news. The loan for the B&B finally came through, right? I know you have connections with some of the employees at the bank."

"Have you talked to Craig lately? I saw him the other day and he asked me about you. Are the two of you getting back together?"

"Craig needs to work on a better apology, and then I'll think about taking him back."

"Don't think too long. I know of at least two women at my workplace who have their eyes on him."

She wasn't going to think too long about getting back with Craig. When he called her again and asked her out on another date, she was going to say yes. She loved her daddy, but guys like Craig only came around once. "I won't, but why do you keep changing the subject? Tell me the good news so I can get started on the renovations. I want to have *All the Fixin'* up and running by the spring."

"Oh, sweetheart," Pierre whispered. She reached across the table and placed her unpolished hand on top of Shea's polished one. "I don't know how to tell you this."

Shea could hear the pounding of her heart in her ears. *No....I can't handle anything else.*

"You didn't get the loan. The bank didn't think you would be able to pay the money back."

"How in the hell can they say that? I only need a small loan. I know they could have given me the money," Shea complained, getting up from the chair and snatched her purse off the floor as tears filled her eyes. "I have to leave. I never thought they would turn me down."

Pierre was beside her in a matter of seconds. "Wait, let me lend you the money and then you can pay me back."

Another handout I don't want, Shea thought. "Thank you, but no."

"Don't leave like this. Let me call Craig. I know he can help you."

208

Great, Craig would love that. She kept pushing him away until she needed the mighty dollar and that's when she would will him back with opened arms. "Pierre, I can figure this out myself," she cried, blinking away tears. "I want Craig back because he's in love with me, not out of pity." She gave her friend a quick kiss on the cheek and left.

* * * *

"Why did that happen to Shea?" Pierre asked, watching her best friend rush to her car parked across the street.

Swinging back around, Pierre started back to her seat when her foot kicked something hidden by the tablecloth. Moving the linen back, she spotted a medium size black book. She flipped through it and noticed it was Shea's diary…correction, journal, as her girlfriend called it.

"I know I should give this back to her, but I'm not. She needs some help and she will get it. It doesn't matter if she wants it or not."

Chapter Thirty-One

"Mr. Evans?"

Craig looked up from the computer screen and the letter he was typing. "Yes," he answered watching the young delivery guy saunter into his office like he owned it.

"I have an envelope that you need to sign." He handed the package along with the pad. "Are you the same Craig Evans that designs the new science fiction website on alienlovers.com?"

"Yes," he replied, taking the package and scribbling his name across the pad.

"Cool ass website. My twin boys love all the colors and how real the aliens look. Do you mind if I ask for your autograph? They will love me if I get it."

"I can do something even better than that." Craig opened his bottom drawer. He pulled out a picture of the most downloaded alien and signed them. "Here you go," he said, handing the man the photos and the pad back. "Let your sons know he's supposed to make a surprise appearance at the toy store tomorrow to promote his new action figure."

"Thank so much. Tomorrow is their birthday and I was still trying to figure out what to get them. This will be the best present." The guy smiled at him and then rushed from his office.

Craig held the package in his hand and turned it over a couple of times before ripping it open. A thick, leather binder fell out, landing with a soft thump into the palm of his hand there was a note attached.

Craig,

Shea, is going to kill me when she finds out I sent this to you, but I don't care. The bank turned down her loan and she's hurting. I know you can help her, but she's too proud to ask you. If you love her, go to her and help her though this.

Pierre

His heart was breaking at Shea losing her dream and it was all because of him. If he hadn't been so wrapped up in *Luscious Lips* staying in the family, Shea would be with him now and working on her bed and breakfast.

Craig weighed the pros and cons of opening the book Pierre sent to him. He had so many good reasons to open it and equally as many to return it to Shea without reading one page. It only took him a matter of seconds before he had his answer, and he prayed it wouldn't cost him Shea.

Chapter Thirty-Two

Shea absently dropped the breadcrumbs at her feet as the ducks came up for their weekly treat. It was one of the coolest days of the year, but she wasn't feeling a thing. All her plans of accomplishing the top item of her five-year plan had failed. She didn't have any other resources.

For the first time in her life, Shea felt defeated and she hated it. She usually saw the glass as half full or the light at the end of the tunnel, but not this time. This bank situation wasn't going to change. She wasn't going to get the money for her B&B.

She didn't have enough credit to get approved for the loan. Why had she allowed her pride to force her into giving Craig all that money back? None of this would be happening now if she kept it and stayed away from him. She was glad he was out of her life.

Girl, be honest with yourself. You miss Craig as much, if not more, than the money you gave back to him.

Shea still didn't know how her relationship with Craig crashed and burned as badly as it did. Did she put too much into it and not allow him to be an equal partner? Did she fall too hard, too soon for him? Whatever it was, she had to figure it out because she didn't want to make the same mistakes in her next relationship.

Why did love have to be so hard? All the times she admired Craig from a distance kept her ecstatic, and it should have stayed that away. It kept her days filled with dreams and her nights filled with hot sinful fantasies.

While she had been back at home her father hinted that he wanted her to work at the family business, but she didn't want to work for him. She loved her daddy, but when it came to his business he was as hard as they came.

Out of nowhere her body grew all hot despite the low temperature of the air, and only one person could make that happen to her.

"I thought I might find you out here," Craig said, standing in front of her a moment before taking a seat beside her on the bench.

Her pulse kicked up another degree at the sight of him wearing a long, cashmere coat and matching gloves. He was simply a gorgeous looking man. "I always come here to think, it's one of my favorite places." She moved her head an inch to get a whiff of his cologne.

"Want to tell me what has you sitting out here in the cold alone in the park?" he asked, taking a handful of bread crumbs tossing them to the ducks. "You know it isn't safe."

"I come here all the time and nothing has ever happened to me." Did he really come here to discuss her safety in the park?

"There's a first time for everything. Why didn't you come to my office and talk to me? You know that

I always told you that you could," Craig said, turning a little on the bench so he was staring at her profile.

"Craig, why are you out looking for me?"

"I have something that belongs to you," Craig slid his hands into the pocket of his coat. He pulled something out and handed to her. "Here you go."

Shea's eyes widened into saucers as she took her journal from him. She didn't even know that she had lost it. "How in the world did you get this?" She placed the journal down next to her on the seat and ran her hand over it. Had he read her most private thoughts about him? Was that the reason he came looking for her?

"Aren't you going to ask me the million dollar question?" he asked, pulling on her ponytail.

"I don't know what you're talking about," she lied.

"Yes, you do." Craig said, taking her hair out of the ponytail holder he ran his fingers through it. "I love when your hair is down. You look so inviting. I can't think of anything else but kissing you."

"Craig, did you read my journal? Is that why you're here saying these things to me, because I know how you really feel about me. Don't forget, I heard you on the phone with Josh."

Groaning, Craig pressed his forehead against the side of her head, "No, I didn't read your journal. As much as I wanted to I didn't read it because it wasn't mine to read," he breathed into her ear.

The whispered words heated up her body more than a caress or a touch from him ever could. "Then why are you here?" she asked, fighting down her desire for the man seated next to her.

"I want to explain that phone conversation you overheard with Josh," Craig answered, moving back from her and taking his wonderful body heat with him. "I want to get the air cleared so we can move on."

"Are you going to tell me that you love me?" she questioned above the sound of her racing heart. "I know what I heard you tell Josh."

"No, I'm not going to tell you that I love you," Craig replied, shattering the last bit of self-respect that she had left.

Why did she ever think she could have a life with Craig? Jumping up from the bench, Shea made her way back towards the walking trail and her car. She wouldn't allow him to see the tears in her eyes. She had that much pride left in her body.

"Damn it, Shea, slow down. I'm not finished talking to you," Craig hollered behind her, but she kept moving. After tossing those hurtful words in her face, what could be possibly have left to say?

A firm hand wrapped around her arm, stopping her in her tracks. "God, woman, why did you take off like that?" Craig demanded, spinning her back around to face him.

"Don't touch me," she snapped, jerking her arm away. "Did you think I would stay after you told me that you didn't love me?"

Wrapping his arm around her waist, Craig anchored her against his chest so she couldn't move. He tilted her head up with his finger. "Shea Antonia Anderson, I'm in love with you. A minute doesn't go by that you don't control my thoughts. I can't get any work done anymore because I'm counting the minutes until I get to see your stunning face.

"When I found out you had overheard me on the phone with Josh I hated myself more than you could ever imagine. Then when I learned you signed over all the *Luscious Lips* stocks to me I knew I lost you, and it killed me.

"My only goal then was to win you back and prove my undying love for you. I would have given up everything for you to smile at me the way you used to. Can you let me slowly earn your love and trust back? Will you let me show you that I'm good enough to be your husband and father of your children? Will you marry me?"

* * * *

Craig stood with Shea enveloped in his arms while he waited for her to answer his questions, but she just stood there staring up at him with those big brown eyes. Memories of his past with Olivia came back full force, and it was scaring the shit out of him.

What if he waited too long? What if she was too hurt by the vicious things he had said about her and she wouldn't take him back. He wouldn't let the love of his life slip through his fingers like this. He would find a way to get through to her. He had come too far to fail like this.

No, he would fight tooth and nail to get Shea back in his life because he didn't want to spend another lonely holiday without her love. The lonely Thanksgiving he spent alone a few days ago shook him to the core.

"Baby, say something," he urged, running his hands up and down her back. "You can't leave me hanging like this."

"I don't know what you say."

"Do you love me?" he asked.

"I've loved you for a very long time, Craig, and you know that. I think the whole town knows that."

Yes! Yes! His mind screamed silently. All wasn't lost if Shea loved him then his careless words hadn't ruined everything, but he still sensed something was holding Shea back.

"What's wrong?"

"Craig, I wanted to have my own success before I got married to any man, and now that dream is gone. I found the perfect house for my bed and breakfast only to lose it. I want to marry you more than anything in this world, but I want us to be equal. I don't want you to be the one taking care of everything, or have the job you love going to every morning," Shea confessed. "Do you understand that I want to make my own mark in this world, too?"

Is that the only thing she's worried about? Craig thought, hugging Shea even closer to his body. "Shea, I know how independent you are, but you're going to have to let your pride go and accept help from the people who love you."

"I know and I'm going to work on that," Shea breathed into his chest, making his blood sizzle in his veins.

"So, let me ask you again, and this time I want a yes or no answer." He moved back from Shea and smiled down into her face. "Will you please marry me and be my partner for life?"

Grinning, Shea brushed her tears away with her gloved covered hand. "Yes, I would love to marry you and spend the rest of my life with you."

Yelling at the top of his lungs, Craig planted a long, wet kiss on her mouth until neither of them had the energy to move away.

"We better leave or we might not be able to make it to the car," Shea sighed, trailing the tips of her fingers down the side of his face.

"I can make it anywhere as long as I have you right beside me," he said, kissing the corner of her swollen mouth, "but I have something I want to give you first."

"Oh, I can feel what you want to give me," she teased, pressing her lower body to his, "however, I don't think this is the proper place for it."

Craig groaned low in his throat, then, took a step back from the sexy bundle tempting the hell out of him. "I'll take you up on that later, the future Mrs. Clark; however, I want you to have this now. Consider it an early wedding gift.

Reaching into his coat pocket, he pulled out a thick envelope and handed it to Shea. He loved the look of surprise on her face. "Here take this. I hope it will make a few things clearer for you."

"What is this?"

"Why don't you open it and find out?" he suggested.

He didn't have to tell her a second time, because Shea's small fingers ripped open the envelope and took out the contents. The excitement on her face made her eyes shine like new penny. Craig waited patiently while Shea read over the documents several times before her eyes jumped back up to his.

"When did you do this?" she gasped, waving the paper in front of her. "How did you have enough time to get something like this done? Is this for real?"

"Right after I got your journal from Pierre and read the note of the top," he confessed. "I have connections and I couldn't let you give up on your dreams."

"I'm really going to have my bed and breakfast, plus all the stocks and money from *Luscious Lips*?" Shea asked again, still in shock from his surprise. "Are you sure that you want to give all of that money up?"

"Baby, I never wanted to be owner of a cosmetics chain, and my aunt knew that. I think she only did that to get the two of us together. We can hire someone to be the CEO for us," he replied as his body felt the temperature start to drop around them.

"Besides, I thought it might be fun for us to have a place to escape to if our day gets too hard. However, since it will be ours we can close it down anytime we want and make love in every room."

"Darling, I like how your mind thinks," she exclaimed. "I can't wait until I make you mine."

"Shea, I was yours the second I saw you climb out of my aunt's pool. I just didn't want to admit it then," Craig confessed, then kissed the woman he loved more than anything in the world.

Epilogue

Dear Journal,

After today I won't have to write in you anymore about Craig, because I finally got him. I just want to say thank you for always being there for me to write in anytime I wanted to. It helped me so much to be able to get my thoughts down on paper.

Rebecca was right. Craig wasn't the man he showed the world and I'm so in love with him. I know that he'll make me happy for the rest of my life.

"You bet I'm going to make you happy for the rest of your life," a hot voice breathed by the side of her ear. "I should have known you would be here, writing in that journal."

Shea spun around in her seat and stared up into the loving eyes of her husband. "I didn't think you would miss me. I saw that you were in a deep conversation with Josh, so I decided to sneak in here for a few minutes," she confessed, then kissed her new husband on the lips.

"Baby, it's our wedding reception. I missed you the second you stepped out of the room," Craig growled, pulling her up from the seat. "How about we ditch these losers and go home? I think I'm ready to start baby making since I want at least three little girls who look like you."

"Are you upset we couldn't take a real honeymoon until next month?" she asked, wrapping her arms around Craig's wide shoulders.

"Mrs. Clark, my honeymoon is any place I get to be with you. I can't wait until we test out that new brass bed at the B&B. Do you think they have it up yet?" He asked as his fingers tried to unbutton at the back of her wedding dress.

"I don't know, how about we sneak away and see?" she suggested, wiggling away from her husband's wandering fingers.

"I love how we think alike," Craig winked. "Do you think the guests will miss us?"

"Let them miss us," Shea exclaimed, then yanked her husband towards the exit side at the back of the church. "We have a new bed to break in."

About the Author

Marie Rochelle is an award-winning author of interracial romance. She is the author of *Caught*, *My Deepest Love: Zack*, and *A Taste of Love: Richard*, all by Phaze Books.

TAKE A FEW HOT
FANTASIES TO BED

PHAZE Presents ...

Fantasies
volume I

four tales of erotic romance by ...
Alessia Brio
Leigh Ellwood
Bridget Midway
Ann Regentin

Presents ...

ntasies
volume II

of erotic romance by ...
Will Belegon
Petula Caesar
Sarah Dickson
Stella & Audra Price

PHAZE Presents ...

Fantasies
volume III

tales of homoerotic romance by ...
James Buchanan
Jade Falconer
Eliza Gayle
Jamie Hill
Selah March
Yeva Wiest

PHAZE Presents

Fantasies
volume IV

four tales of erotic romance by ...
Vivien Dean
Eva Gale
Philippa Grey-Gerou
Cat Johnson

Presents ...

ntasies
volume V

of erotic romance by ...
ictoria Blisse
L.E. Bryce
Kate Burns
Emma Wildes

PHAZE Presents ...

Fantasies
volume VI

tales of erotic romance by ...
Yvette Hines
Augusta Li
Jude Mason
Derek Musgrave
Jessie Verino
and JN

Breinigsville, PA USA
11 August 2010
243416BV00001B/24/P

9 781594 266881